The Cowboy's Christmas Baby

The Cowboy's Christmas Baby

A Grand, Montana Romance

Paula Altenburg

TULE
PUBLISHING

The Cowboy's Christmas Baby
Copyright© 2022 Paula Altenburg
Tule Publishing First Printing October 2022

The Tule Publishing, Inc.

First Publication by Tule Publishing 2022

Cover design by Lee Hyat Designs

ISBN: 978-1-958686-56-0

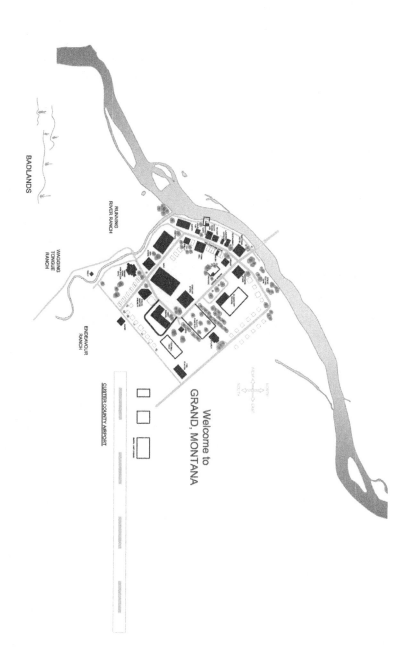

Welcome to
GRAND, MONTANA

BADLANDS

RUNNING
RIVER RANCH

WAGGING
TONGUE
RANCH

ENDEAVOUR
RANCH

CUSTER COUNTY AIRPORT

Dedication

Getting this book finished was a real group effort and I owe thanks to a lot of people. The team at Tule—Meghan Farrell, Sinclair Sawhney, and Roxanne Snopek—were patient, helpful, and understanding. Annette MacPhee-Gallant gave great insights, as usual. And my family is always supportive, especially the Foreign Guy, who has no interest in my writing, hates it when I mention him, but who loves me. Not surprisingly, he knew exactly where I took that wrong turn and got me back on track.

Chapter One

Miles

WHOEVER WAS RESPONSIBLE for the Christmas displays on Yellowstone Drive knew their stuff. From what Miles Decker had seen in the six months he'd been here, Grand, Montana, was as pretty as a picture any day of the year.

But decorated for Christmas?

Amazing.

Glittering lights trussed the underbelly of a black, star-speckled sky. They draped from every tree, shrub, and railing. Every storefront—every business—they all shouted, *let the season begin.*

The only thing missing was snow. They'd had a few skiffs since October, but none of it clung for more than a few days. Miles didn't care much about a white Christmas one way or the other—growing up in Laredo, Texas, he'd seen snow maybe three times, and at Christmas, never—but judging by the conversations he kept overhearing around him, for some of Grand's residents, snow at Christmas was a really big deal.

He'd come downtown intent on buying the perfect gifts for his nephew and niece at the annual midnight craft fair. They'd shut down the waterfront from the town hall to the library. No cars allowed. People flowed freely down the main street, then up the river boardwalk, checking out handcrafted merchandise at the numerous vending stalls.

"Mommy, what happened to that man's face?"

The question, coming out of the blue and uttered in the type of loud whisper only a small child could pull off, dragged Miles's soaring Christmas spirit back down to earth. His head, as if disengaged from his body, swiveled toward the source of that whisper.

His gaze settled on a young mother whose cheeks had gone bright red, likely from embarrassment as much as the wintery cold. A little boy, maybe four or five, clung to her leg. Wide, fearful eyes peered from the tightly laced hood of a navy-blue snowsuit.

"I'm so sorry," the mother apologized. She rubbed the top of her son's head with a gloved hand, whether to comfort or protect him, Miles couldn't say. Either one punched the same blow to his gut.

He summoned an easy smile, the one that used to make women melt, hoping to ease her embarrassment, at least. "It's a fair question." He crouched down to the boy's level, not to get closer to him, but in an attempt to look less… overwhelming. He'd go with that. He tapped his scarred cheek.

"Not very pretty, is it?"

The boy's hold on his mother's leg tightened. He shook his head no.

"It was an accident. My own fault," Miles added. "I've been a cowboy my whole life and I should have known better than to turn my back on a bull."

"Did you shoot it?" the boy summoned the courage to ask.

A perfectly legitimate question. Rural kids knew what happened to animals that ranch hands couldn't control. But rodeo bulls were bred for aggression and that was what Miles had gotten.

"No. The bull was just doing his job. He took offense at me not doing mine right and I got what I deserved."

Miles straightened, tipped his hat to the mother, and went on his way, inhaling the spirit of the season, recapturing the mood, shaking off the encounter.

He meandered the entire square and counted four Christmas trees in all. A Douglas fir monolith, clad in enough twinkling lights to land a wide-body jet, brightened the exterior of Grand's town hall. A balsam fir embraced the front steps of the library. Another Douglas lit up the waters of the Yellowstone River behind the hotel. And the fourth, a Fraser fir dressed in tiny, colorful, shimmering packets of coffee and tea, graced the patio that jutted over the river at the Wayside Café. Every shrub, every doorway, and every rail in the square had been trimmed with ornaments and lights.

He loved looking at them.

He used to enjoy watching kids, too. Their excitement and wonder and pure, simple joy. That was the only thing he missed about being famous—the little ones who all wanted their pictures taken with him, then got so excited they couldn't speak. He'd once been more popular than Santa.

Not anymore. Nowadays, kids took one look at his damaged face and reacted exactly like that poor little guy had—they either burst into tears or ducked behind their mothers' legs for protection.

Strangers weren't so bad. The first time Pax, his three-year-old nephew, hid from him though, he had to admit, it had stung. It might or might not have influenced his decision to stay in Grand for the holidays rather than head home to Laredo, Texas, to be with his family.

He reached the Wayside Café—the last stop on the circuit—and had paused at a stall to examine hand-carved wooden toys when he heard someone call out his name.

"Hey, Miles. Shopping local this Christmas?"

Dallas Tucker, one of the three owners of the Endeavour Ranch, and his fiancée, Hannah Brand, hailed him from across the boardwalk. The pair, without a doubt the cutest and nicest couple in Grand, were snuggled together on a wooden bench. Between them, they knew everyone in town. They were so popular he was slightly amazed to find them alone.

Dallas was a local doctor. He looked more like a recent

college grad who should be backpacking around South America, not wintering in Grand. His black, curly hair was always a few inches too long, as if he couldn't squeeze in the time to get it cut, and he never seemed to pay attention to what went on around him. Looks were definitely deceiving, however. Not much got past him.

Hannah owned the Grand Master Brewery and Taproom. She wore a hand-knit pink toque over long, honey-brown hair, possessed the warmest, most beautiful eyes he'd ever seen, and gave off an air of sweetness that could erode solid rock. She drew people to her—men, women, and children. More importantly, she'd never once looked at him with pity. Envy tickled low in Miles's throat. Women like Hannah had enough sense to steer clear of bull riders.

Rightly so.

He jogged across the boardwalk toward them. "I'm trying to find something special for a three-year-old and a five-year-old. My nephew and niece," he explained, leaking puffs of white breath like a cracked chimney. "So far, no luck. I was about to make another trip around the square to see if there might be something I missed."

"Maybe fidget putty?" Hannah suggested.

"The kids in my practice love that stuff," Dallas added. "Their parents do, too. It keeps little hands busy, and it cleans up easily, so they can play with it in the car on long drives. Or bring it to their doctor's appointments."

"I understand the parental appeal. But my goal is to annoy their parents by setting the gift bar so high it's out of their reach." Maybe make them less scared of him, too. And he still had three weeks until Christmas to make good on his goal.

"Ah. You're a big spender," Dallas said, nodding wisely, as if he wasn't one of Grand's richest residents.

Miles had known Dallas for a little less than six months, but already suspected money was the one thing he knew little about and valued even less. He and Dan McKillop left that particular headache to the third Endeavour owner, Ryan O'Connell. Whereas Dallas, a doctor, and Dan, the county sheriff, were easygoing and friendly, Ryan, Miles's boss, was neither. Miles could never understand why the other two men were so willing to trust him. He wasn't shady, exactly. But he was a man who seemed like he had dark secrets.

Despite that, Miles liked Ryan. He liked working for him. He liked his ambition and drive. Well, he respected them. He only wished the guy would find a hobby that took his attention off the new circuit rodeo and left Miles alone to do the job he'd been hired for. One would think Ryan's pretty, very pregnant, new wife might provide enough of a distraction, but so far, that wasn't the case.

"How's the exhibition coming along?" Dallas asked, tagging along on Miles's train of thought.

Fantastic.

The Grand Chamber of Commerce had no issues with a Christmas rodeo held at the Endeavour, rather than inside town limits. They especially had no issues with Ryan O'Connell.

Miles wished. "We didn't get the permit for a parade through Grand that we asked for." The parade was the throwaway he'd known the Endeavour would never get approved. Declining it gave the chamber of commerce the illusion of power. "But we're going ahead with the fireworks and the dance. They can't stop those. The ranch is private property."

"I don't understand why the town is so set against a circuit rodeo," Hannah said.

"They aren't against it," Dallas explained, proving he really did pay more attention than anyone thought. "They're against the Endeavour hosting it. They think it will eat into the annual horse sale profits and undercut local businesses."

This Christmas rodeo was meant to be a dry run. The real rodeo—the one intended to set them up for the PRCA circuit next year—would happen in February, a few months shy of Grand's annual bucking horse sale held every May. But by hosting a PRCA event at the Endeavour, the town would have little to no say in how it was run, which was what Ryan intended. The chamber of commerce didn't like that.

Hannah rubbed the frost-nipped tip of her nose with a pink mitten. "Why can't the rodeo be part of the horse sale?"

"Because then Ryan would be the one with no say," Dallas replied, again echoing what Miles had been thinking and proving he was nobody's fool.

After chatting for a few minutes, Miles said goodbye to the couple and set off to see if there was anything at the craft sale that he might have missed.

An hour later, he had to concede there was not.

Maybe he was being too picky, he mused as he left the square and its pretty lights behind him, but he wanted to get gifts that suited his niece and nephew. Sydney wasn't a doll type of girl. And Pax? He definitely was not a doll type of boy.

It was going to be weird to celebrate Christmas without them. Kids made the whole season. He should quit being such a coward and go home for a few days. Sooner or later, they'd get used to his face.

If it wasn't for the kids, he wouldn't care so much. His famous face had been a pain in his ass even before it was damaged. For three years, he'd been the public spokesman for professional bull riding. He'd been world champion for the two seasons prior to that. The only person more readily recognized in most parts of the country was the president of the United States. Fame became tiresome pretty fast.

Then, during a photo shoot, he'd turned away from a bull for a fraction of a second, and he'd been hooked in the shoulder and the left side of his face. The angry, red, puckered scar on his cheek ran diagonally from his chin to his temple, narrowly missing his eye, so in that, he was lucky. The scar would fade, although he'd carry it for life.

Plastic surgery had repaired much of the muscle damage. His smile was only a little lopsided and his eye opened and closed normally. He'd been so relieved to discover his shoulder still worked that he'd given no more than a passing thought to his appearance. Still didn't, most days.

But having kids hide when they saw him was unsettling, no question.

He tugged his wool hat over his ears, tucked his hands into his fleece-lined, oilskin coat pockets, and started the long, cold trek to his truck. He might as well have walked to the waterfront from his house because he'd had to park halfway to Billings, anyway.

He found his truck, hopped in, and cranked the heat to full blast. The midnight madness craft fair was misnamed in that it ended at midnight, it didn't begin then. Right now, it was barely ten o'clock on a Saturday night.

Maybe he'd drop in at the Grand Master Brewery and Taproom on the way home and check out if Hannah had any new blondes on tap.

Tate

GETTING SACKED AT Christmas was one more reason for Tate Shannahan to hate the whole holiday season—from the ridiculous store Santa with the fast hands, to the cheap decorations, to the overpriced merchandise.

She fidgeted with the faux-fur-lined hem of the uber-short skirt on her elf suit and tried to pay attention to what her supervisor was saying, mostly out of politeness, and not because she thought she'd hear anything truly constructive. Vanessa Hamilton had been an old lady when they were in high school together and she hadn't grown any younger in the seven years since.

Vanessa leaned across the round, white, cafeteria-style table in the store lunchroom, which doubled as an office. Staff knew to abort if they walked in on a supervisor and an employee in a one-on-one conversation outside of break time.

Like now.

"Maybe you weren't cut out to be a Christmas elf," Vanessa said kindly, as if the two women weren't the same age, right down to the week, month, and year.

Tate couldn't imagine a world in which someone woke up and decided, *I want to be a Christmas elf for the rest of my life*. Then again, she hadn't planned on working as a cashier in a big-box store for more than a few months either, so anything could happen.

The worst part of it was, there weren't many other employment opportunities available in Grand for a twenty-five-year-old high school dropout who'd spent seven years barrel racing on the rodeo circuit. A good grasp of customer service hadn't been something she'd needed.

Knowing how to deal with men and their grabby hands was. A tsunami of indignation swelled, forcing her to restate her side of events. "Santa put his hand up my skirt." Right after he'd badgered her into sitting on his lap to *show the children how easy this is.*

"I understand. But, um, ringing his... jingle bells... might not have been the appropriate response."

There was a better response for being groped?

Tate folded her arms and crossed her legs, bumping her knee on the underside of the table. Her brothers, if they'd seen the battle light up in her eyes, would have advised Vanessa to run. "What was I supposed to do?" *Enlighten me, please.*

Vanessa carried on, blithely oblivious. "Report it to your immediate supervisor—which would be me—so that the incident can be documented. Then, we sit down with human resources to discuss what the next steps, if any, should be."

She couldn't believe what she was hearing. "You're kidding me, right?"

Vanessa was not. "I might have been able to overlook this if there weren't at least thirty kids lined up, waiting to have their pictures taken with Santa, who saw the whole thing."

"You think their parents want them sitting on that creepy old perv's lap after he grabbed my ass? I did them a favor."

Vanessa winced. "I *think* those poor little kids might

have wanted to believe in the magic of Santa a little while longer. At least until after Christmas. Plus, Carl has been our store Santa for thirteen years and we've had zero complaints. Not a one."

Tate found that equally hard to believe. "How many elves have quit on you in those same years?"

"This is *Christmas*, Tate. Show a little holiday spirit and get over it, for Pete's sake. He's a harmless old man from a different generation."

"Just because he's old doesn't mean he can't get a stiffy. If erectile dysfunction is what you meant by harmless," Tate added. "Ask me how I know."

"*Tate.*" Vanessa cupped round, flaming cheeks in her plump, beringed hands. "He says it was an accident. You overreacted. Let's agree to disagree on this, shall we?"

Tate most heartily and emphatically did *not* agree. He'd had his hand under her skirt in front of a crowd of small children while she sat on the same lap they were about to. Why was she being painted the one in the wrong?

But she needed the job—as a cashier, not necessarily an elf—and she wasn't helping her case, especially since some people might argue that Santa had suffered enough. She'd definitely given him reason to think twice about assaulting any elves in the future.

"Why don't we agree that I'll quit the job as an elf but keep the cashier position? In return, I won't file a complaint with human resources and the Department of Labor."

Vanessa was the type to want problems to disappear, not negotiate any terms, and from her perspective, Tate was the problem. Had always been the problem. From grade seven on.

"*You made Santa cry.* In front of *small children*. I can't put you back on cash after that. What would people say?"

Seriously?

"You should be more curious as to what the Department of Labor will say."

Vanessa finally accepted that the problem wasn't going to go away, not quietly and certainly not to her satisfaction. She gave in without grace. "Fine. I'll ask the manager if you can work in the warehouse for a few months until the scandal dies down."

Tate pushed her luck. "Do I get the raise that goes with the change in position?"

"*No.* No raise. You're to be on your best behavior for the next three months. *If* the manager approves it. And you'll have to take customer service retraining. This incident will go on your employee record, too."

Sanctimonious bee-yotch.

"I would love to have this on my employee record," Tate said, with feeling. "Make sure you spell *jingle bells* T-E-S-T-I-C-L-E-S."

Vanessa's double chin quivered. "Your shift is over. Go home."

Tate decided to call this a win. On the positive side, she

would no longer have to listen to seventeen different versions of "Santa Baby" piped through the store's public speaker system. All. Day. Long. And there was always the chance she'd do such a great job in the warehouse that the store manager might move her there permanently.

She had a new problem, however. She'd counted on the extra money that being an elf would bring in to help pay for Christmas. Giving family and friends the perfect gifts had always brought her twin, Tanner, so much joy. This would be the second Christmas since his death, and she was determined to carry on the traditions he'd loved. Last year, wrapped in her own misery and heartache, she hadn't been in a good enough mental place to understand how important it was to keep his memory alive.

Tanner's last, brightly wrapped gift to his girlfriend, Dana Barrett, sat on the shelf in Tate's bedroom closet, reminding her every time she opened the bifold doors that it had yet to be delivered. This year, she'd see to it.

She scurried into the women's locker room—which smelled of deodorant, dust, and decades of despair—to change. She had to swing by the Grand Master Brewery and Taproom, where her older brother, Ford, was tending bar, and wait for a ride home. She wasn't about to show up wearing a forest-green miniskirt and candy-striped tights. For starters, she'd freeze on the walk over.

She caught sight of herself in the full-length mirror next to the staff washroom and stopped in the middle of peeling out of the tights. Hannah, Ford's boss, had said she could clear tables for tips whenever she had to wait for him, and this was a Saturday night. The brewery taproom didn't serve food, meaning the tips were rarely extravagant, and the elf outfit might come in handy.

And with Ford keeping watch from behind the bar, no one would dare put a hand up her skirt.

Not even Santa.

Chapter Two

Miles

MILES HAD A bunkhouse set aside for his personal use at the ranch whenever he needed it, but he'd bought a house in Grand and that was where he preferred to spend his off hours. Since it was only two blocks from the taproom, he left his truck in the yard and walked over.

The Grand Master Brewery and Taproom occupied a weathered brick building that had once been an old dairy. The building itself dated from the mid-1800s when Grand was established. Inside, pub tables with chess boards carved into them butted the walls on opposite sides of the room. Regular tables that seated four people—more, if the people were friendly—hogged the real estate under the street-facing front window. Long shelves held an assortment of board games. A metalwork cowboy riding a bucking bronco hung from the ceiling. Hannah's brother, an artist, had made it for her.

The bar, complete with a brass footrail, squared off against the front window from the back of the room. Right next to the bar hovered a door that led into the brewery itself. Between that magic door and the brewery lurked another, more private, entrance to an apartment above. Hannah and Dallas used the apartment whenever they needed to stay in town for the night—usually when Dallas worked a shift at the hospital. Otherwise, they lived at the ranch.

In a nod to the season, Hannah had spaced red-and-green wreaths along walls netted by colorful lights. Each table supported a cheerful pine bough centerpiece that cupped a battery-operated candle, because drinks and open flames made a bad combination.

While Miles had to work in the morning, he didn't have to make an early start of it. The two Endeavour ranch hands sitting in the corner by the window when Miles entered the taproom couldn't say the same thing. But they were a mere twenty-one years old, eager to enjoy the age of majority, and the long working hours of a ranch didn't stop them from having fun.

He'd been their age once, too, but thirteen years made a big difference in terms of how much sleep he required. He couldn't pass out at the drop of a hat anymore, either.

Now he felt old.

"Handy. Young John." He nodded in greeting. "You boys are out late."

Handy blinked sandy lashes, part drunk, part confused. "It's Saturday night."

Really, really old.

Miles eyed the lineup of empty glasses next to the board game they were playing and decided he might as well roll with the dad—*older brother*—theme he'd begun. "Got a ride back to the ranch?"

Young John, the optimist, spoke up. "Hannah and Dallie might give us a ride. They usually drop in before heading home."

Hannah offered an informal shuttle service to regulars, but she wasn't always around to provide it, so the boys were gambling on something they should have confirmed with her first.

"If not," Miles said, "walk over to my place. You can crash in my living room. I'll take you home before chores in the morning."

"Thanks, man."

The boys returned to their game and Miles aimed for the bar, stopping along the way whenever he was hailed. Most people here knew who he was—this was rural Montana— and since they all lived in the same neighborhood, he'd put in the effort required to learn each of their names.

There was one person new to him tonight, though. A pretty blonde elf, wearing a green skirt that barely covered her perky elf ass, with endless legs sheathed in red-and-white stripes, carried a tray of empty glasses to the bar. She was of medium height and build—curvy but solid, all muscle, not extra weight—and owned an interesting face blessed with angles and edges and full, perfect lips. She bordered on beautiful but came in at a ten due to the sass that flashed in her eyes. It said she'd give a man a run for his money, but he'd likely need a head start to have half a chance. She reminded him of a champagne quarter horse he'd once owned. Skittish and fast and requiring a firm touch. He was intrigued.

But not crazy. She had to be at least ten years younger than he was, maybe more. He'd given up on women like this right about the same time he'd stopped drinking until dawn and sleeping it off on friends' sofas. They'd given up on him the day he'd been gored by a bull and lost his endorsements.

He was good with all that.

He saw Levi Harrington, who worked on the Running River Ranch, sitting alone, and forgot all about the elf. Levi was a scientist as well as a cowboy. He'd studied animal genetics at Columbia University but quit a few years into his PhD program. The two men weren't yet acquainted, but that would soon change.

The Endeavour's plans for a rodeo had several layers to it. Getting it off the ground was phase one. Next up, they planned to breed their own line of bulls and sell them at auction. Miles had suggested to Ryan that, if they were going to engineer their own bulls, it might prove worthwhile to train riders to ride them, too. But that was phase three.

Miles had been wanting to meet Levi regarding phase two for a few weeks now, and this was his chance. He walked up to his table and introduced himself, then pulled up a chair and contemplated his opening line. There was no need to tiptoe around. He preferred the direct, honest approach.

"Word has it you're involved in the Running River's breeding program," Miles said. Word also had it he wasn't happy there. Miles was counting on that being true. "I have a proposition for you."

Levi drank from his half-empty glass. A thoughtful gaze met Miles's over the rim. "I'm listening."

"How would you like to lead a similar program for the Endeavour?"

Interest crackled in the other man's eyes. "I'd have full control?"

That question and the hopeful way it was posed told Miles a lot about Levi's current position. "It depends on what direction you saw us headed in," he replied, careful not to commit. "We'd be happy to hear your suggestions. If we're all in agreement, then the most likely answer is yes. Why not drop by the Endeavour at the start of the new year so we can talk more? In private?"

"I'll think about it."

Which was all Miles could ask. He'd leave it to Ryan O'Connell to sweeten the deal.

He left Levi to his thinking and finally arrived at the bar, where he ordered a beer from the bartender, Ford Shannahan. Santa's pretty blonde helper showed up while he waited. She eased a full tray onto the far end of the counter, then scooted under the flap and began to unload dirty glasses into the dishwasher.

Ford slid a tall glass of cold, frothy, black stout toward Miles before taking his money.

"Who's the new girl?" Miles asked.

"My sister."

Ford's sister, huh? Other than the blond hair and blue eyes, Miles didn't see it. She was sassy and cute. Ford was terse and scary as hell. "I take it by the outfit that she likes Christmas."

A shadow passed across Ford's dour, expressionless face. "Not as much as she used to."

And… there was a story buried in that look somewhere.

One that was none of Miles's business.

The girl looked up from the dishwasher and caught sight of Miles talking to Ford but looking at her. A glass slipped through her fingers and hit the floor, where it shattered, setting chaos in motion. She jerked her arm backward and caught the edge of the tray with her elbow. The remaining glasses sailed off the bar and into the taproom where they landed with a crash. Broken glass scattered at Miles's feet— tiny, glittering pieces of shrapnel.

Heads turned. A few people applauded.

"Damn it all!" the girl swore.

Ford rubbed his forehead and sighed. "Great going, Tate."

Tate Shannahan.

So that was her name.

She grabbed a broom and a dustpan and scurried around to the taproom side of the counter. Her cleaning equipment got caught up in the flap and she swore again as she wrenched it free. Miles crouched down on his heels and began to help pick up the larger fragments of glass.

"I've got it," she said, then glared at the broom as if the whole mess were its fault and it would pay for it later. Stiff yellow bristles scraped against the floor, sweeping slivers and shards into a single pile, the broom no doubt afraid for its life.

There it was—the family resemblance.

Miles sighed, tipped the chunks of glass from his palm into the dustpan, and went back for seconds. He'd never had a grown woman react this strongly to the sight of his scarred face before—at least, not to his knowledge—and he had to keep busy so as not to overthink it. Ninety-five percent of him was as pretty as ever. A lousy five percent shouldn't matter.

"That's the last of it," he said, disposing of a third and final handful of glass, then dusted his palms to make sure he was rid of any clinging bits and pieces. He picked the tray off the floor, stood, and returned it to the bar. Most of his natural charm seemed to have abandoned him, because that was the extent of his ability to get a conversational ball rolling.

Not that she appeared to be interested in idle chatter

with him.

She shifted from one pointy-toed, winklepicker-clad foot to the other, all tense and awkward. Deep, Nordic-blue eyes hit his chest, skated upward, hesitated a split second an inch shy of his chin, then bravely soldiered on.

"Thank you for your help," she said, with the enthusiasm of a sullen teenager forced to thank a great-aunt for the homemade, itchy wool mittens she'd been gifted.

Miles's six senses sprang to life in a very male, very predatory response. The skittishness he'd noted earlier stared him straight in the face. So did a whole heap of wildness. He could literally smell the heat from her skin. A few years ago, he'd have answered the call of the wild, even if only to flirt, but his flirting days were behind him. Especially when it came to flirting with danger.

Danger, in this instance, being her brother Ford, who looked as if he might hold strong opinions concerning men who paid his pretty baby sister too much attention.

She ducked her head and spun away, setting her short little elf skirt a-twirl, and proceeded to rid herself of the broken glass and the dustpan and broom, relegating them to their appropriate places. He kept her in his line of vision, but from the corner of his eye, so she wouldn't notice him watching her.

The polished mirror behind the bar tossed his reflection at him, in case he'd forgotten how important appearances could be. If he turned his head a little to the left, he looked the same as ever. Tilting it to the right, however, was a whole different story. Then, he was no longer Miles Decker, the former face of professional bull riding. He became Miles Decker, the man with the face professional bull riding had ruined.

He picked up his beer, his taste for it gone. Maybe the remaining ninety-five percent of him wasn't so special, at that. Maybe that five percent was a bigger deal than he'd assumed. Because maybe he wouldn't have minded flirting with Santa's pretty blonde helper.

A little.

Miles

MILES ONLY STAYED long enough to finish his beer. Hannah and Dallas had taken the two youngsters in hand so he didn't have to worry about them.

By the time he got home it was dark, bitterly cold, and getting late, and all he wanted was to crawl into bed and grab some much-needed sleep before his alarm clock went off. He started up the short walk to the three-bedroom bungalow he planned to finish renovating as soon as he could work it into his schedule.

He didn't recognize the car parked on the street in front of his house. That was why he paid no attention to it. At first.

Until someone emerged from the car. After that, things took a weird turn. A woman called out his name. She reached into the back seat and pulled out a suitcase.

No, not a suitcase. A baby carrier.

What the hell?

The woman moved under the streetlight, giving him a better look. It took him a few seconds to place her.

Tami. One M, one I. He'd met her back in Texas, at some bar, a few months after the accident. He had a hazy recollection of a mechanical bull, too many shots of tequila, and a motel room where he'd stayed for one night but ended up footing a bill for two weeks.

She hurried toward him. The baby carrier strung from her arms bounced off her thighs. An enormous diaper bag jostled her hip. Meanwhile, uneasiness and a strong sense of foreboding wriggled under his skin.

He'd used condoms. Right?

"I need to talk to you," she huffed, struggling with her baggage, her words turning white in the cold winter air.

Miles eyed the baby carrier, busy doing the math in his head. Whether or not he wanted to hear what she planned to say, or even believed any of it, he couldn't leave a woman and baby out in the cold. "Come on inside."

She thrust the carrier into his hands. A small blanket covered the contents, but he felt it move, so whatever was inside it, it was alive.

He took the bag from her, too. Inside the house, he turned on a light and dropped the enormous diaper bag next to an equally oversized coatrack made from antlers he'd picked up at an auction.

Tami—he had no idea what her last name was—hugged herself and shivered in her thin coat as if she'd never be warm again. She hadn't dressed for a Montana winter. Not in thigh-high leather boots and a short skirt underneath a light, all-weather jacket. Damn, she was young.

He had a mental flashback to Santa's helper. The two women were about the same age. But while Tate Shannahan had a certain untouched innocence about her, Tami did not. When Miles looked in her eyes, he read calculation—and remembered she'd taken him for two weeks' worth of rent as well as a ride.

He didn't bother taking her coat, figuring she'd want to keep it until the heat got through to her skin, then led her into the living room. He set the baby carrier carefully on the carpet and gestured for Tami to take the armchair beside it. The armchair had a woolen throw draped on its arm and she picked it up and wrapped it around her shoulders, over her coat.

No point in dragging this out. No point in wondering what was under that blanket, either. All he really questioned was why it had taken her so long to approach him. "I assume you're looking for child support."

"No." Weariness clung to her. So did determination.

"Her name is Iris. Her birth certificate and everything she'll need for the next few days are in her bag. I wrote down her nap schedule and instructions for feeding."

Money demands, he understood. That was what lawyers were for. He couldn't fully process what was happening here, however, so he asked the first dumb question that popped into his head.

"My name's on the birth certificate?" Could she do that without his consent?

Her eyebrows twitched beneath a fringe of pale platinum hair. Pink lips formed a thin, hostile line. "You're the father. Why wouldn't it be?"

He wished he could be as certain he wasn't the father as she appeared to be that he was. There'd been tequila. A mechanical bull. A night he could barely remember. He did, however, recall the full workup for sexually transmitted diseases he'd had afterward. In detail.

And the two-week motel room bill.

Whether he'd also been set up for a paternity suit or not hardly mattered right now. Babies took two people to make, at least outside of a lab, and in this case, he could very well have been one of the two. He just wasn't sure. Again, that was what lawyers were for.

"I'll have to insist on a blood test," he said.

"You do that." She shrugged out of the blanket. "My number's in the bag along with the instructions for her care. If you decide to put her up for adoption, let me know and

I'll sign whatever paperwork you need."

Adoption?

What the hell kind of extortion was this? What kind of mother was she?

"Why are you doing this?" Miles asked, too bewildered to put up a fight. This was a *child* they were discussing. A human being. A life. "If you need money, I'll give it to you. Once the blood tests come back, then we'll talk about child support."

"I don't want child support." She waved a hand around the living room of his fixer-upper. "I can do better than this." *I can do better than you*, her tone further implied. The look she cast him was full of pity laced with a faint trace of revulsion that he didn't miss, either. "But not with a baby holding me back. I carried her for nine months. I've looked after her for eight more. As of right now, she's all yours."

She left without so much as saying goodbye to her daughter. There was no backward glance. No signs of regret or remorse. Short of wrestling her to the floor and tying her up like a roped steer, there wasn't much Miles could do to stop her.

He heard the front door open and close. Then he heard himself breathing. Felt his pulse hammering against the cuffs of his sleeves. He leaned forward to give his fogged brain a chance to recover from the sudden shift in blood pressure.

Had a woman he'd only known for one night just abandoned a baby with him?

Miles, you dumb bastard. Why on earth should this come as a shock? He'd known the risks. He'd even warned younger riders who were new to the circuit to watch out for the buckle bunnies hanging around. But he might have gone a bit crazy for a while after the accident, not sure of what the future might bring.

A small, kitten-like sound cut through the whirring noise in his head, and the blanket covering the baby carrier moved, ever so slightly. Slowly, carefully, as if approaching a live hand grenade due to explode any second, he tugged the blanket aside.

And was greeted by a fluffy tuft of brown hair crowned with a hopeful pink headband that served no real purpose other than as a decoration. Wide, solemn eyes blinked against the sudden light before focusing on him. A tiny nose quivered above a cute pair of buttoned bow lips, their owner undecided as to whether she should burst into tears.

He knew the feeling.

They stared at each other. Miles was no stranger to babies. Loved them, in fact. He'd been hands-on with his niece and nephew, adoring them from day one. But this was the first time he'd ever found himself saddled with the sole responsibility for one.

The enormity of it struck terror in him. He'd rather get back on a bull. What did he do if she got sick? Who did he call?

Call Dallas Tucker, you fool. He's a doctor. Get your shit

29

together and think for a second, why don't you?

He massaged his forehead with the heel of his hand. First things, first. The baby—*her name is Iris*—appeared to be in no immediate distress, so he dug through the diaper bag to see what else Tami had left him. Formula, cereal, diapers, a few changes of clothes… Ah. Here it was. A notebook with a birth certificate clipped to the cover.

Miles examined the certificate. Iris would celebrate her eight-month birthday in three days. No father was listed. Didn't that figure?

Why had Tami only come to him now, after so many months?

Logic suggested the long delay stemmed from indecision as to what her best prospects might be. Once she found out Miles's endorsements had truly ended, she'd likely decided it was best to cut her losses and move on.

If the paternity test came back positive—and there would be a test—then the joke was on her. He'd carefully invested his money for years. He was no billionaire, not like the Endeavour's owners, but he was a whole lot better than comfortably off. He'd kept a tight lid on his finances for this very reason.

"Well Iris, it seems we're roomies," he said. "Let's get to know each other better, why don't we?"

He unfastened the straps on the carrier and lifted her into his arms, half-expecting her to start screaming, but it turned out she was tougher than that. She eyeballed him as if she wasn't sure what to make of him, but whatever else he might be, apparently, he was no threat. She wore a soft pink onesie and smelled even better than his truck when it rolled off the lot.

She was a real beauty. She didn't look much like her mother. She did, however, look like photos of Miles's sisters when they were babies. He could see a little of Pax in her, too, and Pax looked like him. Her eyes held a flush of baby blue but were definitely darkening to green.

And then the little imp smiled at him, all gummy and toothless, and he thought his heart might explode. The thrill of excitement laid a beating on any remnants of terror. If this was his reward for drunken errors in judgment, then he couldn't say he was sorry. The paternity test would be for his lawyers because he was already convinced.

He had a daughter.

Chapter Three

Tate

"I HEARD MILES Decker is looking for a babysitter," Maybe said.

Tate choked on a mouthful of coffee.

The two women occupied a small table for two near a glass door overlooking the waterfront at the Wayside Café. Inside, wall-to-wall strands of Christmas lights sparkled. Thick fronds of pine garland draped along the tops of the pastry display cases. Cheery candle centerpieces brightened every flat surface. Hints of ginger, cinnamon, and apple flavored the air. Early morning frost, not yet killed off by the sun, slicked the twinkling wooden boards of the patio outside.

Still no snow, however. Not that Tate cared. Nothing good had come out of Christmas in over two thousand years and definitely not in the past two.

Her friend Maybe—AKA Mabel, although very few people dared call her that to her face—was the youngest of three sets of identical twins. Maybe was distinguishable from her counterpart Meredith—known in the family as Mayhem for reasons that became more apparent as one got to know her—primarily through personality, rather than appearance. They were tall, curvy, chestnut-haired beauties with striking, golden-brown eyes. Even Tate, who'd known the twins since they were five years old, sometimes confused them. To further complicate things, all six sisters looked alike. Tate's brothers used to tease Maybe that her parents had to be first cousins for their gene pool to replicate with such precision.

"Why on earth would Miles Decker need someone to babysit him?" Tate managed to croak once her fit of coughing subsided.

"Miles doesn't need babysitting, idiot. His little girl does."

Miles Decker had a daughter? How was it possible for her to not know this?

Tate had followed his career with the rabid fervor of a tween Shawn Mendes fan. She'd kept a poster of him on her bedroom wall until she left home at eighteen. She'd known all his stats. She'd dreamed of becoming a bull rider on the off chance she might meet him someday. And when she'd finally met Miles in person?

She'd made a complete fool of herself—but not for any reason her tween self would understand. She'd taken one close-up look at the damage done to his face and the dangers of the sport came crashing back on her, along with the memory of her twin brother's poor, broken body, lying unmoving in the arena. A cold fist had grabbed onto her lungs and twisted until she couldn't breathe—not a full-blown panic attack, but close to it.

She'd had two major attacks since Tanner's death—both of them when she'd tried to approach an arena. They made her so angry… She was stronger than that.

"You should apply for the job," Maybe added.

And Tate was in need of a new one. While Vanessa hadn't been brave enough to fire her, it turned out the store manager wasn't at all worried about silly little things like the law.

"*We've had eleven complaints about you so far,*" he'd said when she showed up for her shift, because apparently the whole town was less interested in Santa's behavior than hers. "*Plus, your supervisor claims you've been difficult to work with from the day you started here.*"

Thank you, Vanessa.

Which was why Tate was sipping a spiced pumpkin latte with Maybe and listening to Taylor Swift Christmas songs at the Wayside rather than ringing in sale items on cash.

"I can't babysit for Miles Decker. I already told you. I embarrassed myself in front of him at the taproom."

Maybe rolled her eyes. "So you broke a few glasses. He's likely used to women getting all clumsy around him."

Undoubtedly true. What woman wouldn't go nuts? Miles Decker was one of those men who owned any room he walked into. Attention automatically defaulted to him.

Women loved him. Men admired him. The scar on his left cheek merely added to the mystique. It certainly wasn't the first thing people noticed about him.

Plus, he'd insisted on helping her clean up the mess she'd made, proving that not only was he beautiful, but he was also a gentleman. Despite his reputation. Which raised even more questions.

Who was the kid's mother? *Where* was the mother?

Maybe provided the answer without Tate having to ask. "Rumor has it a woman showed up out of nowhere and dropped the kid on his doorstep. Ten-to-one says she's some buckle bunny who gambled and lost. Miles would have lawyered-up. Hard."

Those odds sounded about right. Lots of women hung around rodeos, hoping to rope the next rising star. Even Tate, while never a true buckle bunny—not with Tanner around to make sure that didn't happen—had been a big bull rider groupie, herself.

Now her hands got all sweaty and she dropped trays of glasses simply because Miles Decker happened to look her way. It made her angry. And scared. And even more angry. None of which she'd admit. Not even to her best friend.

"I don't know anything about kids." Other than they didn't like it when Santa Claus cried. "Besides, dozens of women have probably already applied."

"There's only one way to find out." Maybe snatched up Tate's phone. She punched in a number while slapping

PAULA ALTENBURG

Tate's hands away.

Tate heard the phone ringing, then a smooth, familiar, male voice.

Oh, my God.

"Hi," Maybe said into the phone. "This is Tate Shannahan. We met the other night at the taproom? I heard you need a babysitter and I'd like to apply. Uh huh. Uh huh. Yes, I have experience." Maybe listened intently. Tate heard the smooth rumble of Miles's sexy voice on the other end of the line but couldn't make out any words. "Sure. Of course. Eleven thirty is fine. I'll be there."

She thumbed the disconnect icon and tossed the phone toward Tate. "You're to meet with him at the Endeavour's main office at eleven thirty. Walk in the front door of the ranch house and he'll be in the common area, waiting for you."

"You're a horrible person, Mabel," Tate said. She tucked the phone in her purse, where it would be safe—although too little, too late.

"It's only until you find something better. And I bet he pays well."

What could possibly be better than working for Miles Decker? Her starstruck, tween inner self jumped up and down in excitement.

"What if he hears what happened with Santa?" Tate didn't think she could survive having the face of bull riding think poorly of her. She got enough of that from ninety-nine

36

percent of the town.

"Pull yourself together, woman. So what if he does? Do you think *Miles Decker* will care that you set Carl Beaman straight for putting his hand up your skirt?"

Maybe was probably right. Despite his dog reputation, Miles had always been a vocal advocate for women in an industry where women had to look out for themselves. One more reason for women to love him.

"You told him I have experience with kids."

"It's not rocket science," said the impatient woman with a horde of nieces and nephews she largely ignored. "Play a few games. Watch television. I hear shark babies are in. Feed her spaghetti and hotdogs. That's what we grew up on. Besides, what other employment options are out there for you right now?"

Maybe was definitely right about that. Tate was twenty-five and owned not one single marketable skill. Barrel racing used to be it, but she'd loved her horse more than the sport and had to quit after the sight of the arena made her pass out. She'd just gotten fired from a job most sixteen-year-olds could handle. She lived in a double-wide trailer owned by her brother.

She would have lived with her parents, but they sold the family home and moved to Florida shortly after Tanner, the family golden boy, died. When she suggested she spend Christmas with them, they'd made excuses as to why Christmas in Florida wasn't for her. She'd gotten the message. They'd never come right out and said it, but they blamed her for Tanner's death, too.

Now her best friend expected her to humiliate herself further in front of Miles Decker. Her hero. By showing up and having him turn her down because she wasn't even qualified to babysit. Hadn't she suffered enough?

"Babysitting is perfect for you. You've always liked taking care of other people, Tate. Face it. You're bossy. And you've been lost ever since..." A brief, delicate pause suggested Maybe couldn't find the right words. "This will give you a purpose until you get back on your feet. You can't live off Ford forever."

Maybe was right yet again. Tate had to make some sort of plan for her future, and to do that, she needed money. Besides, her inner tween self really, *really* wanted to work for Miles Decker. Where was all that self-confidence she'd once possessed?

"Okay. I'll go to the interview. But I'm blaming you if I don't get the job and my self-esteem is destroyed."

"That's the spirit. Think positive," Maybe said, toasting her with the dregs of her latte.

TATE AND FORD lived about ten miles outside of Grand, putting her halfway to the Endeavour Ranch's main house, which was twenty miles out.

She'd bought an old car with the last of the money from selling Davey, her quarter horse, before moving home. She'd loved Davey. But the mare had begun showing her age, and with her barrel racing days pretty much over, she deserved a better retirement than Tate could afford. Trained barrel horses, particularly ones as twitchy as Davey, weren't suited for children, so Tate had sold her to a small, reputable ranch that planned to use her for cutting cattle and breeding. Tate hadn't visited, even though she was welcome, because she didn't know if she could walk away from her twice.

She passed through the Endeavour Ranch gates and coaxed her tiny car up the long drive. She parked next to an enormous garage, then crossed the yard to the front door of the hotel-sized main house, where a sign on the door told her to enter. She knocked to announce her arrival, because she was intimidated as hell and it was the polite thing to do, then pushed the door open.

Someone at the Endeavour liked Christmas. A lot. A star perched atop a giant fir tree stroked the ceiling some twelve feet above. The tree's density and girth alone inspired awe. Delicate strands of light twinkled off the hundreds of crystal ornaments weighting its branches. A seven-foot angel crafted from iron watched over a metalwork nativity scene set up next to the tree—an incredible piece of art. She couldn't begin to imagine how much it must have cost to create such a display.

Meanwhile, she'd bought her coat secondhand three seasons ago and her jeans were torn at the knees—through wear and tear and not by design. She was so out of her class. She should never have come. But she had and it was too late to run. All she could do now was fake it, so she swung her jaw closed and forged onward.

Miles was right where Maybe said he would be, in the center of a common area complete with leather sofas and stone flooring. He was on his hands and knees, crouched low to the floor, growling as he touched noses with a tiny human who was growling back at him. Tate's heart turned to goo. This had to be the sweetest sight she'd ever seen.

Miles spotted her and bounced to his feet like the former athlete he was. "Tate. Thanks for coming."

God, he was beautiful.

And then he smiled. It distorted one side of his face. The room slid sideways and started to spin, but this was one of the milder attacks, and the pounding in her chest wasn't so bad. The solid floor under her hadn't budged, meaning she could control it.

She focused on Miles's eyes, not the scar, and took a few deep, grounding breaths. The room settled back into place. The heaviness behind her breastbone eased off. She tucked her shaking hands into her coat pockets. Only a few seconds had passed.

"That's a baby," she blurted out, because she had to say something—anything—to cover up her weird behavior. She was now two-for-two as far as making a fool of herself went.

You'll pay for this, Maybe.

"Yes, she is," Miles acknowledged, his probing eyes attempting to lock in on hers. "Is that a problem?"

It was. It so was. He had no idea. Babies probably didn't eat hotdogs.

"Not at all. I love babies," she replied, all enthusiasm, even though she had no idea how she felt about them, because she'd never actually interacted with one before. A brief stint as an elf was as close as she'd gotten.

This one was cute, though. She had a tuft of brown hair that looked like a worn, patchy carpet, chubby little legs that couldn't possibly support her body weight, and a pink romper adorned with red hearts. The booties on her tiny feet were cute, too, but Tate doubted very much if they were meant for hiking. They looked more like mittens for toes.

The innocent smile was what did it for Tate. The tiny tot had inherited her own brand of charisma from her larger-than-life dad. She rolled to a sitting position on her puffy behind and grinned. An open expression full of self-confidence proclaimed, *the world loves me and you'll love me, too.*

Oh, sweetheart. If you only knew what a cold, hard, cruel place the real world can be.

This little darling needed someone to protect her from a world filled with ranches, rodeos, and cowboys, and that someone was Tate. She had tons of that kind of experience.

So how did she fake childcare experience, of which she

had none?

"What a doll!" She scurried past Miles and homed in on the tot, her brief flare of panic forgotten. *Work with me, kid.* She scooped the baby up by the armpits, which seemed to go over well, and perched the diaper-clad bottom on her hip. She stroked a plump cheek with one fingertip. They regarded each other with mutual suspicion, but Tate persevered. "What's your name, gorgeous?"

"Iris," Miles supplied, sounding as dazed as his young daughter appeared.

"Well, Iris," Tate gushed, even though, with those green eyes, the baby was grossly misnamed. *Fern* would have been a much better choice if they were intent on a botanical theme. "You and I are about to become buddies. How old is she?" She fired the question at Miles.

"Eight months tomorrow."

"A party is in order, then." *Oh, the fun.* Tate had lost track of her high school friends—other than Maybe—but knew of at least five who'd gotten married. Surely one of them had kids by now. She tried to recall if Maybe's married sisters had any babies Iris's age.

"I'm less interested in your party-planning skills than I am in whether or not you can change a diaper," Miles said, interrupting her thoughts. Alarm replaced the stunned look in his eyes and warned her she was trying too hard.

"It's been a while," she said, dialing her enthusiasm back to something less weird.

"Why don't we find out how good your memory is?"

"Okay, it's been never," she was forced to confess. There was no reason for Iris to suffer all because she hadn't known there'd be a test. "But I'm willing to learn. Changing diapers won't be the hardest thing I've ever done."

"Fair enough. I'll walk you through it the first time and we'll see how you do. Follow me."

She carried Iris, who arched her back and stiffened her legs as if she knew what was coming and had already decided it wasn't for her. Miles led them to one of the public restrooms close to the main door. It had a big plastic change station attached to one wall.

Tate held Iris at arm's length and examined her pink romper, which had holes for her arms, legs, and head, but no exit that she could determine. He'd offered to walk her through it, but she hadn't intended to ask for his help quite this fast. Now, if she were saddling a horse...

But she wasn't. "How do I get her out of this thing?"

Miles leaned against the bathroom door. He lifted one eyebrow. "How do women get in and out of a teddy?"

Tate blinked. "Do women even wear teddies, anymore?"

"Yeah," Miles said, the curve of his lips and faraway look in his eyes giving up way too much information as to how he could be so sure.

"I think my grandma might have owned one," Tate replied, because really. There were some things about Miles Decker, Rodeo Star, that she did not need to know, and how he'd spent his nights on the circuit was at the top of her list. She liked to cling to her preconceived notions.

He shrugged and folded his arms. Chest muscles rippled under his long-sleeved, navy T. "You could call her to ask how they work. Or, you could give it your best shot and figure it out on your own."

So much for walking her through it. He wasn't trying to be any real help at all. Tate took a closer look at Iris's outfit. She spotted a flash of shiny metal. "Well, I'll be darned. It snaps at the crotch."

Miles shook his head in purse-lipped despair. "This is not going well."

Not really, no. "Give me a minute. I'm not done."

She now had nothing to lose. Iris was as wriggly as a fish on a hook, but Tate managed to get her romper unfastened without her flipping off the change station and onto the floor. She inspected the waistband of the diaper, searching for clues. "These tabs peel off, right?"

"Yes. Here's a tip. You can lift her up by the heels—but only enough to slide the dirty diaper from under her and a fresh one into place."

"In other words, no swinging her around my head like a lariat?"

"I'd prefer that you didn't."

He sounded as if he thought she might actually be serious.

"Oh, come *on*." Tate rolled her eyes at him while keeping a firm hold on his squirming bundle of joy. "Give me some credit. I may not have changed a baby's diaper before, but I do have common sense."

"I believe you." His tone added, *right*. He passed her a disposable diaper. "Wipes are beside you."

After a few more false starts, and some more-or-less helpful coaching, Tate finally got Iris diapered and the romper refastened.

Miles rolled up the wet diaper, packaged it into a compostable bag, then tossed it into a gleaming, stainless-steel garbage can with a lid. "It's not the most environmentally friendly diapering method, I'll admit, but disposables are better for Iris right now. Me, too." He grinned at Tate, who held Iris. "I've changed more diapers in the past two days than I have in my whole life, so I'm no expert either. You did okay."

He didn't cause a panic attack, exactly, when he looked at her that way, although the fluttering behind her breastbone returned. Her fifteen-year-old self would have died on the spot. Her twenty-five-year-old self merely slid in and out of a coma and lost the use of her tongue.

What a beautiful, beautiful man.

But she'd apologize to Santa before she ever let on how excited she was at the prospect of working for him.

He held the bathroom door open for her so they could return to the lounge. "I have a schedule written out," he continued, walking behind her, thankfully unaware of his effect on her. "I'll bring her to the ranch with me every day. The owners have said we can use this area as a playroom. Ryan and his wife are expecting a baby in February and that's what they were already planning to turn it into. They work right over there." He gestured toward two glassed-in offices at the far side of the room. "I'll buy more toys. Right now, we're making do with what Iris has until I can find time to go shopping for baby things."

Gradually, from the things he was saying, Tate came to understand she'd been hired. She was going to get to work here, in this beautiful room, surrounded by all these shining, beautiful things. It almost made her like Christmas again. Best of all, she'd be working for *Miles Decker*, who she'd adored from afar. Until now.

He talked on, making more plans, saying she could eat at the cookhouse if she liked, and also, that he had the use of one of the bunkhouses if she'd prefer to put Iris down for her naps there. "But she sleeps like she's hibernating. I doubt if the light traffic in here will disturb her," he concluded.

"Don't you want to check my references?" Tate blurted out, because she'd never learned how to quit while she was ahead.

"I already checked them. After you called, I contacted Ford to find out why his sister was interested in babysitting. Ford seemed surprised and said you already have a job, so I called your workplace, where your former boss told me you'd been let go this morning. Which concerned me, so I called

46

Hannah Brand. Hannah told me she'd heard from Diana O'Sullivan that you'd had an altercation with the store Santa, which likely led to your dismissal. When I spoke with Diana, she said she'd taken her kids to the store for pictures with Santa and saw the whole thing. So did half of Grand, by the sounds of it. Both women gave you their stamp of approval."

"Santa had it coming," Tate muttered, her outrage over being fired for defending herself at war with pleasure that she'd been given a good reference in spite of it all.

Miles clapped his hands over Iris's ears, bringing him a few steps closer to Tate, who still had the baby perched on her hip. "It's Christmas. Let's not speak ill of Santa. Carl Beaman, however, from what Diana says, is getting a lump of coal in his stocking."

"It isn't funny," Tate said automatically, because privately, she was dying inside that she'd get to work for her hero. This was going to be so much better than retail.

"No," he said, agreeing with her. He lifted Iris into his arms, although Tate found she gave her up with an astonishing regret, considering the two had only just met. "But you could have filed a complaint with the sheriff's department if you felt that strongly about it. Dan McKillop's a good guy. So why didn't you? File a complaint?"

A good question. Except women didn't do things like that in Grand. Dragging the law into it would have been the cheap and dirty approach—the one a tattletale took. Plus, if she complained to anyone, it would have been Ford. And Santa, while creepy, didn't deserve to die.

"It wouldn't have changed anything other than to make me look like I can't take care of myself."

"Taking care of yourself is that important to you?"

It was important that Ford didn't have to. He had enough weight on his shoulders.

"Every woman should know how to be strong," she said.

Miles held Iris tighter and kissed the top of her tufted head. "That's definitely something I intend for my daughter to learn." He smiled at her and the fangirl in Tate almost fainted. "How about we see you tomorrow morning?"

The scarred cheek, while noticeable, wasn't what left her speechless. His eyes were amazing. Green, flecked with gold, and circled by rings of rich, creamy chocolate. She could gaze into them all day long.

She shook off her stupor. She had a new job. With Miles Decker, no less.

And oddly enough, thanks went to Santa.

Chapter Four

Miles

"THEIR TOP BUCK-OFF rates average just under sixty-three percent, but they'll do for a family event," Miles said, offering his official opinion of the six bulls due to be brought in for the Endeavour's rodeo to his boss.

The two men were in Ryan's office in the main house, going over the rodeo program. Prize money would be awarded, but since the one-day event was not PRCA-sanctioned, no participant's standings would be affected if the bull they drew underperformed. This Christmas rodeo was strictly to show off the venue, and the Endeavour owners had sunk a great deal of cash into getting the new arena ready. They had their judges lined up—two for the timed events and four for roughstock. Four professional bullfighters had been hired, including a barrelman who'd dress up like Santa to entertain the kids in the crowd.

Thinking of Santa made Miles think of Tate Shannahan. If Hannah and Diana hadn't given her such warm recommendations, he likely would never have hired her. Not because she'd pinched Santa's jewels. Kris Kringle got what he deserved. And not because she stared at his face. While disconcerting, that wasn't a problem for him. He knew how he looked. Not even because she had temptation written all over her, and he had no time or patience for that, anymore.

He couldn't quite put a finger on the real source of his reservations. She was maybe a little too star-struck, perhaps. A little too impressed by his name. Too eager to please. Her perky enthusiasm—*let's plan a party!*—made him feel old and tired. And getting fleeced by Iris's mother was still fresh in his mind. *What a rookie mistake.*

A few discreet questions had uncovered more of her story. She'd been a barrel racer—a decent one, by all accounts, although not necessarily destined for greatness—and barrel racers didn't have the best reputations when it came to steadiness and reliability. They tended to be buckle bunnies, too. Except Tate didn't really give off that type of vibe.

Tate's twin brother, a bull rider who'd showed promise, but still green enough that he hadn't hit Miles's radar, had been the real star in the family. From what Miles understood, he'd moved up in competition a little too fast and ended up on a bull he couldn't handle.

"Miles?" Ryan lifted his brows. "You with me?"

"Sorry, I missed that," Miles said, because his boss's lips were moving but not one word had sunk in.

To his credit, Ryan kept his annoyance in check. Marriage had mellowed him, for sure. "I asked if you were going to ride in the rodeo."

"Afraid not. I'm out of practice, and I'm still competitive enough for that to matter."

Longing tiptoed inside him, but when he'd quit, he'd sworn that was it. He wasn't going to become a crippled old man, limping around the arena, reliving his glory days to anyone who'd listen, all because he'd powered on past his prime.

Ryan eyeballed him as if he were crazy. The two men weren't so far apart in age. But Miles had plenty of scars and knobby, knitted bones to guarantee aching joints on cold, rainy mornings already.

"You've got two weeks to get back in shape," Ryan said. "It's not as if you'd have real competition. Not at your level. The other riders who've signed up are all amateurs."

"So far." The sign-ups were in, but there could be last-minute changes.

It was tempting, though. He didn't really care about the competition part of it. He could play to the crowds one last time and it would all be in good fun. The proceeds were earmarked for charity. Plus, these local bulls were hardly top tier. More and more, based on what he was seeing, Miles believed the Endeavour's plans for a breeding program could prove successful, especially if they brought Levi on board.

But if he rode, it would be because he was chasing the thrill, not his pride. Nothing beat an eight-second ride. He'd never be old and tired enough to forget that.

"I'll think about it," he said, when he should have said no.

Ryan's eyes fixed over Miles's right shoulder on the glass wall behind him. Miles half-turned to see what had hijacked his attention.

Tate, her blond hair tucked under a bright purple tuque, looking frost-nipped and lovely, struggled with the heavy door and the stroller. She tried to push the awkward rig forward over the threshold, when the best approach was to drag it behind her. He itched to jump up and go help, but she'd proven herself perfectly capable over the past several days and didn't need help from him. She'd figure it out.

Iris's round baby cheeks glowed bright pink from the cold, matching her snowsuit, which was puffy enough to wedge her upright in the stroller. She bounced up and down, with a big smile on her face, as if having the time of her life.

His heart grew three sizes. He couldn't believe how lucky he was to have this little sweetheart come into his life, and for Christmas, no less. Even though he'd like to believe he wasn't really a Grinch, he'd been feeling that way. The holiday would mean nothing to Iris—she was barely eight months old—but it meant a whole lot to him, especially this year, because the decision as to whether he should go home to Texas had been made for him. No way was he flying with a baby he didn't yet have clear title to. Plus, his scarred face made it impossible for him to travel without the world knowing, and he didn't want to subject her to public attention when she was so little.

Part of him worried that her being handed to him was too good to be true, and she might be taken away, even though Ryan had used his connections to confirm Iris's mother was indeed out of the picture and unlikely to return. The DNA test Dallas had ordered was for Miles's own peace of mind. He'd love Iris regardless, and was already attached, but while possession might be nine tenths of the law, parentage made up an irrefutable ten percent.

Tate finally wrestled the stroller inside, caught sight of the men watching her struggle, and waved. Her warm, unfiltered smile rivaled Iris's and made her look equally sweet. He could see why Carl Beaman had assumed she'd be an easy target for a quick touchy-feel. *Good for you, Tate.*

He'd have no complaints if a little of her sass rubbed off on his daughter. A girl really should know how to look out for herself, something he'd never had to consider, before.

"How's Tate working out?" Ryan asked, since they were both staring at her.

The other man's interest kicked Miles's territorial instincts into gear, which completely uncalled for, considering Ryan was a happily married man with a beautiful, equally happy, pregnant wife.

Ryan was a definite predator, however. Not in the Carl Beaman way. But he sniffed out problems the way a wolf scented blood and his method of dealing with them could be equally cold—which was why the local chamber of commerce preferred dealing with Miles.

"So far, so good." Tate was a fast learner, and when it came to children, a natural. She and Iris had definitely clicked.

"We'll need someone to help Elizabeth once the baby is born," Ryan continued. "Think Tate will stick around long enough for that, or will she head back to the circuit?"

It was a really good question and echoed his own concerns. He could personally attest that the urge to compete remained strong, even at the tail end of a successful career, and Tate was young. She'd been on her way up, not out, and while he didn't know much about babies or how resilient they were, he wasn't sure having Iris bond with her was a great idea so soon after she'd lost her mother. She didn't need to lose a caregiver, too.

But Tate's barrel racing career wasn't why Ryan was curious about her. He'd talked about setting up childcare onsite for the ranch owners and staff, and he was always extra cautious about the people he hired. He didn't like lawsuits, and rich men were targets—didn't Miles know it. If Tate worked out well, he wouldn't have to go through the trouble of hiring someone new when his own baby arrived.

"Hard to say at this point," Miles replied cautiously.

"Understood." Ryan kicked back in his chair, signaling that their meeting was over. "You got everything you need?"

He meant for the rodeo.

"Yes." Miles relaxed now that Ryan's attention had shifted from Tate. He had local sponsors lined up for each event and award. He'd recorded a local radio spot for publicity, and it played often enough that he was tired of hearing his own voice. Staff were hired to help with operations and the dozens of administrative tasks that kept cropping up. Entry fees were already in and the stock contractor's delivery date for the bulls was confirmed. He checked his watch. "I'm off to the arena for a final safety review of the stadium seats with your engineering consultant."

He closed Ryan's office door behind him, entering the lounge. Every time he came in here, he found something new. Today, it was a life-sized, old-fashioned red sleigh filled with gaily wrapped boxes. Next year, Miles would have to tie Iris from the ceiling to keep her from getting into this stuff.

Dallas, Hannah, and Elizabeth were responsible for the Christmas decorations, with help from Dan's sisters and mom. They were like little kids let loose in Santa's workshop. Elizabeth really wanted the teenagers in the group home she ran as part of the Endeavour's community service program to experience the joy of the season, although the kids hadn't acted especially joyful when she insisted on them decorating the tree.

His niece and nephew would love everything about this, from the decorations to the atmosphere of anticipation to the candy and fudge scattered around the room in beribboned glass dishes, and that caused a pang of regret. He loved those two little bugaboos as much as he loved his new daughter, but with Iris now in the picture, the decision not to go to Texas for Christmas was final.

He stopped to check on her on his way through the lounge. She lay on her back on the floor, with Tate peeling her out of her snowsuit, while she gnawed on a teething biscuit, turning it to mush in her tiny hand.

"You, umm… You have cookie goo. Stuck in your hair," he said to Tate, waggling a finger at the sticky blond tresses, fighting hard to hold back a grin in case he was the only one who thought it was cute. Women could be unpredictable when it came to their looks.

"It's not the worst thing I've ever had stuck in it," she replied with a complete lack of concern, which made sense to him, since she'd worked around horses. He'd been coated in a lot worse than cookies in his career, too.

She combed her fingers through the shiny blond locks, plucking out as much of the damp mush as she could, and while he avoided thinking about how pretty she looked, he thought of something else he hadn't considered until this very second. She hadn't signed up for the barrel racing event. Why not?

Maybe she assumed she wasn't eligible because she was working for him. Maybe she couldn't afford the entrance fee, what with it being so close to Christmas. Maybe he was being nosy and wanted an excuse to ask whether she'd quit the circuit for good or was merely taking a break.

Mind your own business, Miles.

"I'm headed down to the arena to wait for an engineer," he said. "Would you two young ladies care to join me?"

Tate rocked back on her heels, flipping her semi-cleaned hair over her shoulder. "You really expect two gorgeous young ladies like us to hang out with an old geezer like you?"

Her sassy mouth was as hard to resist as Iris's baby-toothed smile. The lift of her chin added a dash of flirtiness to her words, and he lost his hold on his grin. It charged out of the gate and latched onto his cheeks. "Old geezer, huh? Now my feelings are hurt."

She tickled Iris under her chin. "Do you hear that, sweetie? He really is an old geezer. He's trying to guilt trip us into doing what he wants."

So that was how Santa had convinced her to sit on his knee. He'd wondered.

"Or," he said, deciding he'd better speak up in defense of old geezers worldwide, because they weren't all like Santa, "maybe I'd like to spend time with my daughter while I've got a few extra minutes. And maybe I thought you might like a guided tour of the new arena, too. You're a barrel racer, aren't you?"

"I used to be."

Which told him nothing, other than that it was a subject she didn't want to discuss, meaning he had to pursue it rather than leave it alone. "The Christmas rodeo is for charity and we don't have many barrel racers signed up. I'd be happy to sponsor you if you want to compete. You'd be doing the Endeavour a favor."

Tate's lovely face lost a little of its shine. "It's hard to compete without a horse."

He'd stepped in that one. Had she been forced to sell hers? Maybe that was why she no longer rode the circuit— she couldn't afford the upkeep after her brother was killed. He didn't dare offer to find a ride for her, which might only serve to rub salt in a wound, but he supposed this answered his question as to whether she'd leave to go back on the circuit.

If she did, it wouldn't be anytime soon. A quality barrel horse would be hard for a serious competitor to replace, and Tate didn't seem all that serious about it.

He reached for his daughter. "Why don't we get Iris zipped back into her suit and go take that tour?"

Tate

TATE FASTENED HER jacket and wrapped her scarf around her neck, going through the motions, dragging the process out for as long as she could.

She'd been doing so well, not thinking about today, focusing on the baby and the activity around her.

But she'd dreamed of her brother last night. Tanner, wearing his vest, chaps, and a wide, happy grin, with his bull rope in hand, leaned against the rails of the arena in Calgary, Alberta. She felt the heat and smelled the dust in the air, a dry combination of animal dander and droppings. The sun and the wide blue prairie sky were behind him. He hadn't qualified and was simply watching the competition, not the least bit concerned that he wouldn't move on. He turned his head and looked directly at her.

"*Life is short, Tate*," he said, and his happy smile broke her heart. "*Enjoy it.*"

Life had no business being that short. Not for someone who loved it so much.

She had no desire to go anywhere near the new arena. Not today, of all days. Already, she felt the hot coals of anxiety burning inside her chest, exacerbated by the horrifying possibility that Miles might notice. She could inhale shallow breaths, but had trouble letting them out, leaving her light-headed and dizzy.

She'd researched panic attacks online and understood that arenas were triggers for her, thanks to witnessing Tanner trampled to death in one. The attacks crept up on her—they didn't announce themselves so she could prepare—and she couldn't stop them once they took hold. She had, however, been working on techniques to help walk her through them.

But touring the arena on the anniversary of the accident wasn't going to be easy. She focused on breathing from her belly—*in for four seconds, hold it, then out*—and forced her muscles to relax, starting with her toes and moving upward in sequence. She silently chanted her personal mantra. *You're strong. You got this. You're strong. You got this…*

But she didn't. Not with her hands shaking this hard. Not with an audience, either. And especially not when that audience included a man who didn't know the meaning of fear. Every day, when he looked in a mirror, he faced a reminder of how dangerous bulls were, and yet here he was, on a ranch every day, working with them.

"I have to make a pit stop." She struggled to sound as though her heart wasn't trouncing her ribs and her lungs weren't on fire. "Go on without me. I'll catch up."

Miles jiggled the bundled-up baby nestled in the crook of his arm, humming "Jingle Bell Rock" under his breath, making Tate want to scream. Iris patted his nose with a tiny red mitten. He reached for the door, letting in a cold blast of fresh air, paying no attention to Tate, his attention utterly absorbed by his daughter.

"Don't forget the stroller," he said. "You'll likely want it because I'll be stuck at the arena for most of the day."

She'd worried for nothing that Miles might notice something was off. When his daughter was around, he only had eyes for her. And while, normally, Tate loved to watch them together, right now, she wanted him to hurry up and get out.

She waited for the door to fully close behind him, then darted into the bathroom and paced up and down until the fire in her chest burned itself out and she could breathe normally again. She splashed cold water on her face and wiped it dry with a paper towel.

Then, she faced herself in the mirror—the same way Miles did, every day. She hadn't seen any evidence of triggers in him.

"I cannot change the past. Only the future," she intoned as she met her own eyes. "You've seen the inside of dozens of arenas, so get out there and take that tour. Get it over with and the next one will be easier."

The dread in her stomach remained, but at least the anxiety had passed. She forced herself out of the bathroom and through the front door, grabbing the stroller on her way out. She clattered it along the path behind the house that led to the dome-shaped arena to the right of the barns, grimly gripping its handlebar. *Breathe from your belly...*

It was barely ten o'clock in the morning and the day hadn't warmed up in the least since she and Iris had come in from their walk. The sun glowed white against a vibrant, cloudless blue backdrop. The frozen ground remained bare. It could well end up a green Christmas—which was less than three weeks away. She stubbed the toe of her boot against a small stone and sent it scuffing ahead of her down the path. Had Dana signed up for the Endeavour's Christmas rodeo?

Somehow, Tate had to work up the nerve to deliver Tanner's final gift to his girlfriend. She and Dana had been sitting together when he'd been thrown. Dana's screams still rang in her ears.

As she approached the arena, she saw none of the normal

bustle she associated with it, which took the edge off her anxiety. No fans or competitors. No dusty odors of horses and cattle. No noise or confusion. One lone half-ton truck was parked near the loading bay doors where stock contractors would drop off livestock for the scheduled events in a few weeks. Gradually, her tight lungs relaxed.

She walked through the spectators' entrance and deposited the stroller beside the ticket booth. Wreaths of fresh pine and red ribbon adorned the draped walls of the concourse encircling the arena.

The soles of her boots tapped the concourse's polished concrete floor as she followed the sound of male voices. She found Miles and Iris outside one of the vendor stalls, speaking with Raiden Strong, owner of a local agricultural equipment dealership.

Even though the arena was unheated, Miles had taken his jacket off and hung it over a railing. Iris appeared to be quite content in his arms. Her snowsuit was unfastened to the waist, and her mittens, strung together by yarn, dangled from empty pink sleeves. A knit cap covered her wisp of hair. Rosy cheeks and bright green eyes shone with contentment. Tate couldn't decide which one of the pair was most appealing. They both made her heart quiver.

She pulled out her phone and snapped a picture of father and daughter together.

"Hi, Tate." Raiden grinned broadly at her as she joined them. "I hear Santa will have to sit on an ice pack when he takes his sleigh ride Christmas Eve."

Raiden was one of Ford's friends. Normally, Tate liked him. Right now, she couldn't think why. She lifted her eyebrows, pinched her lips between her teeth, and tilted her chin. "And let that be a lesson to Santa to keep his hands off his elves."

"He should have known better than to mess with you, that's for sure."

Tate was about to remind him that, while Santa putting his hand up her skirt was bad enough, doing so in front of small children was even more wildly inappropriate.

But then Raiden risked his own life by adding, "Ford is one scary dude. He should hope no one tells him."

Raiden, you ass. "Really? Being afraid of my brother is the biggest reason he should have known better?"

Raiden's gray eyes grew wary. "I didn't know this was going to turn into a multiple-choice quiz or I would have kept quiet."

Miles finally weighed in. "Santa took advantage of a situation by banking on Tate not making a scene. Santa was wrong on both counts. Let's hope he learned a lesson." His voice was quiet, but nevertheless, filled the arena. Iris, one thumb in her mouth, remained mesmerized by her dad. She hugged his waist with her knees and dribbled wee fingers along his scarred cheek.

Raiden, who really was decent, knew when to admit to a mistake. "Sorry, Tate. It's just that Carl is an old man.

Chances are good his filter is slipping, and he lacks impulse control."

That possibility had already been pointed out to her, and while age wasn't much of an excuse in her books, her real anger was reserved for the store and its management. No matter what, she wasn't the one who'd deserved to be fired. "Even more reason why Carl should hang up his suit."

"You're right," Raiden said. "I know the store manager. I'll see that Carl isn't asked to be Santa next year."

Tate had so much to say about patriarchism, no matter how well intentioned, and where Raiden could put his. She opened her mouth to begin, but Miles gave her shoulder a squeeze, either as a warning or a show of support, maybe both.

"Let's take that tour," he said to her, nodding a friendly dismissal to Raiden, who appeared more than ready to find better places to be, so she let it drop.

But as they prepared to walk through the arena, with Miles eager to show her around and share its finer features, she discovered one positive thing had come out of her vexation with Santa and old boys and their networks.

Most of her earlier anxiety was gone.

Chapter Five

Miles

SEEING THE ARENA decked out for Christmas raised conflicting emotions in Miles. Part of him couldn't wait for the day of the rodeo. Another part of him wallowed in bittersweet longing for his mom's turkey dinner.

This year, bonding with his sweet little daughter and putting her needs first trumped all the sweet potato pie in the world. He'd make Christmas special in Grand. Not so much for Iris—she was too little to notice or care—but for him. She gave him a reason to put up a tree. He'd test drive new traditions with her in mind.

She'd fallen asleep with her head lolled against his shoulder and her warm baby's breath dampening the side of his neck. Her limp arms dangled like the reins of a riderless horse. Despite the sleepless nights, and disposable diapers that were a lot harder to dispose of than the ads would have people believe, he was in love.

"This is the sound booth," he said to Tate, carefully opening the door to a small room and sidling in so as not to disturb Iris. The booth was situated at the far end of the arena, away from the chute, but mid-row in the stadium seating, looking down. A large window overlooked the arena. "This is where the sound guys and lighting technicians work their magic and wind up the crowd. We have a laptop with touchscreen, a digital console, and over here, we have a tablet linked to a Wi-Fi router that allows the sound engineer to roam the whole arena if he needs to."

"Oh my, look at all those switches," Tate murmured politely, in that lilting tone of voice women adopted when they were humoring men.

A laugh bubbled against the backside of his ribs. He'd felt a tad sorry for Raiden, who'd been on the verge of getting a taste of what Santa had suffered, which was why he'd run interference. What had surprised him, however, was that Tate hadn't picked up that Raiden was trying to impress her, even if he'd gone about it all wrong. How had she spent so much time around men on the circuit and remained so… unaware?

Tanner Shannahan must have been equally as scary as their older brother, was all he could say. However, in his opinion, her overprotective brothers had left her vulnerable, no doubt the opposite of what they'd intended. Her pretty blond looks, sweet smile that gave even Santa ideas, and bold, saucy mouth would pose a challenge to any man not as decent as Raiden. Silvery gray ringed the deep blue of her eyes. His gaze drifted lower. She had curves in all the right places and in proportions he liked—none of them over or under done.

And he had to ask himself—in all his years in the spotlight, what type of man had he been? Early on in his career, how would he have viewed a woman like Tate? Would he have treated her with the respect she deserved? Or would she have been nothing more than a challenge to him?

He liked to think he would have been respectful, but the truth was, he didn't know.

He flipped a few of those switches she'd disparaged. Seconds later, Gwen Stefani was belting out "Last Christmas" over the speakers throughout the arena while colored lights flared.

"You're a Gwen Stefani fan?" She sounded so surprised.

"You know someone who isn't?" he countered, enjoying her disbelief. Let her see there was more to him than an ability to stick a ride and smile for a crowd.

"I guess that's true if you're into pop," she conceded. "I'm trying to imagine Kaleb Driggers roping a calf to this... Who'll pick the Christmas rodeo soundtrack?"

What was he doing, flirting with a girl too young to know about Gwen's ska punk beginnings?

"I'll leave that to the professionals." Since rodeo music was matched to the moment, it took someone who knew what they were doing to get them paired right. "Besides, I'm not so much a fan of Gwen Stefani as I am of Christmas," he added. "My family's big into it. I'm a little sad not to be heading home to Texas. This'll be the first one I've missed."

The thought of his mom's face when she found out he wasn't coming gave him all kinds of guilt. He hadn't told anyone about Iris yet, either. The family thought he was delayed because he was working. He didn't mind missing Christmas Eve mass quite so much, not being especially religious, but he did love the tradition and being reminded of what the season was really about—peace on earth, good-will, and all that.

Tate's eyes turned to bright, sunny skies. "What's stopping you?" Then her gaze drifted to Iris, asleep in his arms, and he realized the conclusion she reached when those twin skies clouded over.

"I'm not ready to drag a baby through airports," he said, nipping off her line of thought before it took root. Embarrassed about Iris? Not in this lifetime. She was perfect. Any dad would be proud. He wasn't sure what made him add the next part. Probably because he'd never seen the slightest trace of pity in the way Tate looked at him. "I've never especially cared what people think of my face. Not before the accident and not after. But I care what kids think. The last time my three-year-old nephew saw me, he cried and hid from me."

"My friend Maybe's youngest niece cries and hides when she sees her, too," Tate said. "Maybe's pretty enough. She's just mean. Ever consider that a little facial scar might not be your real problem?"

A laugh burst out of him, disturbing Iris, who puckered

her mouth and frowned in her sleep. "You think I'm mean?"

Tate studied his face in a way that he liked—nine-tenths admiration combined with a touch of honest assessment. She wasn't a woman who knew how to keep her thoughts to herself. "No. I think Maybe's mean. I think you're worried about nothing. The scar will fade and your nephew will get used to it. But he can't get used to it if you stay away."

"You're probably right."

Her hands went to her hips. Her chin lifted. She cocked her blond head to one side. "You *know* I'm right. Which means we're back to Iris being the reason. Are you telling me that Miles Decker—world bull-riding champion three years in a row and former national spokesperson—can't manage air travel with one well-mannered baby?"

Laughter threatened again. Tate and her unfiltered opinions had him justifying himself and his decisions more than he normally would. He'd never explained Iris's sudden appearance to anyone, figuring it was nobody's business, not until now, as he witnessed every question and conclusion that raced through Tate's head. *Who was the mother? How well had he known her? How stupid was he?*

Pretty stupid, as it turned out.

And he still had no regrets.

"I also thought I should wait until the paternity test results are in before I try taking her out of state," he said.

"She's definitely yours." Tate dismissed science with one lift of a blond brow. "She looks too much like you for there to be any doubt about that. And since her mother left her with you…" Thank God, she kept her opinion on *that* to herself. Pretty blue eyes bored into his. "Does your family know about her?"

"Not yet." And, yes, he knew that was wrong.

"Pretty big secret. Are you worried about what they will say?"

"*Hell*, yes." His dad, in particular. He'd never liked Miles's reputation with women. "But it will have nothing to do with Iris. They're going to love her." Which was the absolute truth. Another grandchild to spoil? They'd be all-in. But enough talk about him. "What about you? What are your plans for Christmas?" he asked.

Just like that, Tate's lovely face lost its light and its sass. She ran a finger along the edge of the audio mixer, avoiding his eyes. "My mom and dad moved to Florida this past year, so it's just me and Ford. He says he's going to try cooking a turkey, but I think we both know how that will end up. His cooking skills are no better than mine."

She said it lightly, but Miles wasn't fooled. Ford, he could understand not making a big deal about Christmas. The guy was borderline grim and born to play Grinch. But Tate, with all her cute, *let's throw a party* enthusiasm? What about that? He'd have thought she'd be all over Christmas.

The horseshoe dropped. He really was stupid. The Shannahans had buried their brother at Christmas. Not much wonder Tate had such a hate on for Santa.

Miles had a big heart. It hurt for her. Ford, too. The season was about peace and goodwill. About life and hope and family and friends. He held Iris tighter. His daughter was going to grow up knowing those things. Next year, for sure, he was taking her home.

This year, he wanted to start new traditions. He wanted this to be their home—the one Iris longed for after she grew up and moved away. Why not make Christmas a little bit better for Tate while he was at it?

"The Endeavour's Christmas party for family and staff is Friday night," he said, since she hadn't been working for him very long and might not know she was included. "Are you coming?"

She looked away. "I thought I'd help Ford at the taproom and earn a little extra in tip money."

She'd never make money at poker, that was for sure. Not if this was the best she could do. The taproom would be closed because of the party, to which Ford had also been invited, not that anyone really expected him to attend.

Tate, however... Why wasn't she interested? "What... I don't pay you enough?"

She cast him a slight smile in response to his feeble attempt at persuasion. "You pay me plenty. But I've never been much of a saver and it's time to start, because I can't live with Ford for the rest of my life. He has his own plans."

"I see. You're at a crossroads. We all go through those." He nodded in understanding. "There will be lots more of them, too."

"Says the old geezer." She cracked another smile, and his breath tickled the inside of his chest, right where Iris's tiny body was currently warming his heart.

"That's 'wise old geezer' to you." He settled a hand on his daughter's back. "I'll need help with Iris, since she's coming, too, so the gig pays. Plus," he added impulsively, "I could use your help in picking out the right party dress for her. I know how important these things are to women. Want to go shopping with us after I finish up here for the day? I should be done around four."

Indecision flickered in and out of her eyes, mixed with something that might be confused with relief, before her sass reasserted itself. "Do I get paid time and a half after hours?"

She wasn't serious, but she should be, because it was a reasonable request. "Of course." He'd throw dinner in, too.

"Then I know where all the best-dressed babies in Grand do their shopping," she said.

Tate

IF NOT WANTING to sit home alone on the anniversary of her brother's death made Tate a coward, so be it. She'd never claimed to be perfect.

She could have called Maybe for company, or any other

friend, but found she preferred spending the evening with someone who didn't know what this day meant to her. Ford, of course, was working and even if he wasn't, their shared grief wasn't a topic of conversation. She cast a sidelong look at Miles, in the driver's seat of his truck. It didn't hurt that she'd crushed on the someone in question for years, even though he'd made it quite plain that as far as he was concerned, she made a better playmate for Iris than him. The nine years, two months, and three days between them did seem like a lot, but a little fantasizing about him was harmless enough.

It wasn't as if a difference in age was what really put him out of her class. Take his truck for example. She'd never seen the inside of one quite this fancy before, let alone ridden shotgun in it. Black, leather-wrapped steering wheel, matching bucket leather seats with bright-orange stitching, sound system to rival that of the arena, and a computer screen mounted on the dash... It smelled delicious. Straight out of a showroom.

Iris was strapped in the back seat of the double cab, wide awake after the long nap she'd taken, but content to gaze at her surroundings while amusing herself. She babbled in a language only she understood, and which required no response from the adults in the front. She was so easy to care for that Tate almost felt guilty taking money from Miles. How could her mother abandon her? How could anyone not love her?

Tate had known plenty of women who believed babies were better than lottery tickets. Iris had likely cost Miles a fortune—not that he seemed to care—but it didn't make her feel good about taking his money for a job she'd do for free if she could afford to.

"So where are we headed?" Miles asked, sounding as cheerful as his good-natured daughter. Not much wonder Iris was always so happy—her dad scattered contentment the way flower girls sprinkled petals at weddings. Iris's mother was an idiot if she thought money was worth more than this.

"Jax in the Box," Tate said. "It's a high-end children's store, specializing in custom clothing. A friend's mother owns it and sews everything herself. She also buys it back on consignment and resells it as 'gently used' because most of it is only ever worn once or twice before it's outgrown."

"Does she have time to whip up something new before Friday?" Miles sounded doubtful. "That's less than two days."

Tate had no idea. She did know that Maybe's mother had repurposed more than one of Maybe's outfits for Tate. And that he'd completely disregarded what she'd said about consignment. "Does it have to be new?"

He looked at her as if she'd suggested he pluck something out of the trash. "I can't dress my daughter in castoffs."

Tate shook her head, a little annoyed, both with him and herself, because his words nicked a nerve. Every decent piece of clothing she owned came secondhand, including the jacket she wore—although pride kept her from pointing it out. "Wait and see what she's got before you pass judgment."

The puckered scar tissue on his cheek bobbed in startled affront. "I'm not a snob."

"Of course you're not," she said sweetly, even though it was exactly what she'd meant to imply. Just because he was famous didn't mean he had to act like he was, too. Living in Grand would poke all kinds of holes in his ego.

"I'm not," he insisted.

"Sure." She patted his arm. "I believe you."

That slow, sexy grin reemerged—the one that sparked heat in places Santa had not. "You're messing with me."

"Maybe a little." The bridge that spanned the Tongue River and led into Grand appeared ahead. "I do think you should see what Jax in the Box has to offer before you make a decision."

"Point taken."

They turned right onto Marion Street and passed the Grand Home for Special Care before reaching a strip mall a few hundred yards beyond it. A sign at the parking lot entrance advertised several local small businesses, including Jax in the Box, but the Rage Room was the one that set local tongues wagging. Tate had heard plenty about it, but so far, hadn't tried it herself. Its target market was mostly stay-at-home moms with pent-up frustrations to vent. Grand had an abundance of those.

Miles was out of the truck and around to Tate's side before she could get a foot on the rubber-gripped-steel running board. Warm hands caught her waist under her jacket and steadied her while she disembarked. She didn't have time to become flustered by the unaccustomed assistance before he dove into the back seat to free Iris, who'd been his real goal.

Tate had been in his way.

That was all.

And it was so sweet. The sight of father and daughter together like this always turned her insides to goo.

"She has a stroller," Tate felt obliged to remind him, because he seemed intent on carrying the poor child everywhere. If he kept this up, Iris's first date was going to be so awkward.

Miles grinned at his daughter, who grinned right back at him. He shifted that wide grin to Tate. "I bought that stroller for you. She weighs next to nothing for me."

"Testosterone… what a wonderful gift to mankind," she said, rolling her eyes, because otherwise, they'd all end up smiling like idiots and the two women entering the Rage Room might lose their incentive.

"I disagree. I'd have to say the gift is for women. Would you rather do the heavy lifting yourself or have it done for you?"

"Having a choice would be nice. Some women find fending for themselves empowering."

"In my world, the women hold all the power. My job is to serve them." Miles gestured for Tate to precede them.

"After you, She-Ra."

Princess of Power. Cute.

Spending the evening with Miles and Iris was so much more fun than sitting home by herself, feeling sorry and sad, that Tate almost felt guilty for enjoying herself today, of all days.

And then, in her head, clear as a bell, she heard Tanner's voice. "*Life is short, Tate. If you really want to have a choice about something, why don't you choose to be happy?*"

Hearing his voice, as if he stood right here beside her, took her out at the knees. She staggered and would have fallen if Miles hadn't caught her.

He stooped and peered into her eyes, concern edging his. "Hey. You okay?"

Other than an acute case of embarrassment and an overactive imagination?

She swallowed hard and forced herself to say something light. "Tell me you aren't used to women throwing themselves at your feet."

"Well, yes. But not literally. When did you last eat?"

"I had lunch." Lack of food wasn't her problem, but having him think she'd almost passed out from hunger was preferable to him thinking her crazy.

He kept his hand on her elbow, no doubt to be sure she didn't face-plant on him, but she really was fine.

"Dress shopping, then supper," he said, his tone letting her know that the decision wasn't up for debate.

Since Tate only had frozen french fries and chicken strips waiting for her at home, she didn't argue.

Cloda Quinn, Maybe's mother, was another of Grand's many huge Christmas fans, it quickly became obvious to newcomers, if they'd had any doubts. A fat, gorgeous pine tree, trimmed with angels and lace and red ribbons, hogged the front display case in a position of glory. The shop reeked of ginger and spice and everything nice thanks to handcrafted, scented candles strategically placed to satisfy whatever fire marshal happened by. Bing Crosby and David Bowie's "Little Drummer Boy" assaulted Tate's eardrums. Cloda's paying customers were well past their toddler years, so when it came to her shop music, she favored the sentimental seventies and eighties.

And Cloda loved fashion. With six near-identical daughters to dress, she'd developed an obsession for giving them each something different that suited their personal tastes. She'd turned her obsession into a commercial success.

Cloda's once-dark hair had lost its battle with gray, and fine lines crinkled her eyes and her lips. She had what Maybe lovingly called a "mom" body, with a hint of middle-aged spread she made no effort to hide. Her red wool cardigan, black turtleneck, and tailored black trousers announced comfort was as important to her as style. Leather, stack-heeled, lace-up ankle boots decked out in a red floral pattern shouted that an attention to detail was a far better weapon against aging than a few nips and tucks.

She worked at a sewing machine in a corner of the cluttered shop, intent on a piece of navy-blue fabric that looked like velvet, but Tate knew would be machine washable and virtually indestructible.

"Tate!" she exclaimed, catapulted out of her chair when she looked up and saw who'd arrived. She hurried over, wrapping Tate in an enthusiastic embrace. "How are you, my love? You doing okay?"

Tate's chest ached in response to the question. Cloda knew what day today was.

"Fine," she replied brightly, wishing people would quit asking her that. *Whatever are you talking about? No issues here.*

She glanced at Miles, who was rescuing a red sweater from Iris's sticky grip.

Cloda's eyes narrowed, not fooled for an instant. "Any word from your parents?"

The band of ache in her chest tightened. "No."

Cloda hugged her again, longer and harder. "Give them time, sweetie. You and Ford are adults and they know you have plenty of support here in Grand. That frees up their mental space for them to battle grief in their own way."

So far, their battle involved looking for others to blame and they'd settled on Tate. She'd been the bossier, more dominant twin, older than Tanner by five minutes, the one who'd gotten them both into trouble from the day they'd taken their first steps.

"This is Miles Decker," Tate said, desperate to turn the

conversation to something less painful and private, especially after the incident outside. "He's looking for a party dress for his daughter."

If Miles had been listening to the conversation—although how could he miss it—no one would know what opinion he'd formed. Tate envied him that particular talent of keeping his thoughts to himself. He leaned forward, arm outstretched, amiability oozing from him like slow-flowing lava.

"I'm so pleased to meet you," Cloda said, shaking his hand. "Tate and my daughters have followed your career since your first ride. They're all huge fans. And you must be Iris," she added, proving Grand's gossip mill was nothing to sneeze at. She wobbled one of Iris's wee boots, knowing better than to gush all over a baby before she was ready, and received a sweet smile in return. "I assume the dress is for the Endeavour's Friday night Christmas party?"

That last question was directed at Miles, who nodded, and Cloda got straight down to business. She posed a dozen more questions before steering Miles toward the gently used rack, which was where Tate had warned he'd end up.

"I completely understand wanting her to have something made specifically for her," Cloda assured him, as if his concern for an eight-month-old's fashion sense would make any difference in what she planned to sell him. "I raised six girls—three sets of identical twins—and believe me, being environmentally conscious while taking individual personalities and tastes into consideration was a challenge. Continues to be. But I firmly believe that we have a duty to this planet and the generations to come. Jax in the Box endorses that belief. My mannequins have worn these dresses longer than any child ever has, and when the clothes come back to me, I take them apart and remake them. I also have a line of practical clothing for older children that are made completely from recycled material and are durable enough to survive outdoor play in Montana. Those items usually get passed on to younger family members and friends instead of returned."

"Three sets of identical twins?" Miles sounded dazed, fixating on that as if it was all he'd absorbed from Cloda's enthusiastic barrage of ethical baby couture information.

"It's rare, but not unheard of," she confirmed, blissfully sifting through a rack of tiny, lace-trimmed dresses until she found what she sought. "Tate's a twin, too. Of course, she and Tanner were fraternal." She tugged a cranberry-red dress with a bib of white lace from its hanger and held it up for Miles to inspect. "This is the right size and was only worn once. The deeper red will be perfect with those pretty green eyes."

Exactly whose pretty green eyes she referred to Tate couldn't be sure. Not after the wink Cloda gave her. She felt her face take on the hue of the dress. Cloda knew she'd had a thing for Miles Decker, the professional bull-riding champion. But Tate knew the difference between a famous persona and reality, and Miles Decker the father only had eyes for one lucky girl in the room. Tate wouldn't dream of encroaching on that fledgling love. The pair made a super-cute couple.

"Is there a factory leaking twin-producing chemicals into the local water supply around here, by any chance?" Miles asked, ignoring the dress—which really did look like new—and also the wink, for which Tate gave thanks.

Cloda laughed. "Not that I know of, and contrary to Grand speculation, my husband and I aren't first cousins, either. We hit the baby jackpot three times, but family luck must skip a generation. So far, out of seven grandchildren, none are twins."

Watching Miles discuss his options with Cloda, decide on a dress, then tiny white cotton tights and a cute pair of shoes to go with it, only confirmed for Tate that when her teenaged self had needed a hero to worship, she'd chosen the best. She let her thoughts drift while Alan Jackson sang "Holly Jolly Christmas" for all it was worth. Teenaged Tate would be in her glory right now.

Why don't you choose to be happy?

Because grown-up Tate knew happy endings didn't exist. All of this bright Christmas cheer only lasted a few weeks at best before the world lost its magic and reverted to normal. Unfortunately, she didn't know what normal was anymore.

Back in the truck, with Iris safely strapped in her seat and the shopping bag stowed behind Tate's, Miles started the engine. He looked over at Tate, wearing such a thoughtful expression that alarm settled in. She didn't want to be one of those women who threw themselves at him. She wasn't that obvious. Was she?

But the gut-punch he delivered was of a far different kind.

Chapter Six

Miles

M ILES HAD SEEN plenty of bulls with that exact same look in their eyes—a cross between panic and anger, and a need to tear into something, but not knowing how, when, or where to begin. Then, all hell would break loose.

Which wasn't what happened here. This was much worse, because hell was what he would have expected from Ford Shannahan's sister, and a bull rider's twin, and the woman who'd crushed Santa's 'nads.

He only had a hazy idea as to what stages there were to grief, but it seemed to him that Tate had progressed beyond rage—although without a doubt, red-hot embers remained—and now somehow seemed lost.

Why wouldn't she be? If he'd understood Mrs. Quinn correctly, her family was broken. The Shannahan parents had completely disengaged from their remaining two children. He couldn't imagine such a rift with his own tight-knit clan.

"Losing a twin must have been hard, especially at

Christmas," he said.

Tate's gaze broke from his. She picked at a fingernail with her thumb. "Christmas didn't have a whole lot to do with it. Seeing him trampled to death with no way to stop it would have been hard no matter what time of year it was."

Ouch. She'd been in the arena, and didn't that suck? The scar the sight would have left her with would be a lot harder to deal with than the bit of damage done to his face, and he'd bet she was a whole lot more traumatized than she'd have people believe. Sympathy would likely only earn him what Santa had gotten, however. He didn't know her very well yet, but self-awareness wasn't shaping up to be one of her strengths.

"Yes, I suppose it would be hard any day of the year," he said, and left it at that. Iris began to fuss in the back seat, reminding him that he had two girls to feed because he'd promised Tate supper. "Let's go grab something to eat at my house. I'm glad you don't have any quarrels with Christmas," he added, "because I have a tree to trim and could really use your help."

"You put up a tree?"

He shifted the truck into gear and backed out of his spot. "Millions do. Why wouldn't I?"

"I don't know. It's just…"

She floundered, and he heard what she'd thought better of saying—because it wasn't what she'd expected of Miles Decker, whose manly image his publicity team had gone to great lengths to protect. For a woman who had issues with gender inequality, she sure held onto a few biases of her own.

"More work for an already too-busy guy?" he suggested, helping her out.

"Exactly."

She was cute. Prickly as a porcupine, but cute. Especially when she flashed that quick, gut-knotting smile. It gave him the same thrill he got from one of Iris's equally genuine, equally unfiltered, grins. It was also the same thrill he used to get when he drew a bull outside of his comfort level, which should serve as a warning. If Tate were a bull, she'd be named Trouble. Or Trainwreck.

The drive to his house was short, but he took it slow because he wanted to check out the neighborhood competition as far as light displays went. Next year, he intended to win. He'd have to keep an eye on the McIntyres, he decided. They'd put serious planning into their yard display. Their power bill had to be fierce.

"Look what you've done with the place!" Tate exclaimed, admiring the paint and new floor when they finally walked into the house. Then, she ran a hand over the coatrack made of antlers. "This is… unusual."

Which was woman-speak for *isn't this ugly?* meaning maybe he should rethink its location. The ranch bunkhouse might be a better place for it. "You've been here before?"

"I used to date a boy who lived here. But that was years ago. I didn't know the family sold it." She hung her coat on the rack and straightened her cropped sweater, which had hiked up to her ribs, revealing a small silver stud piercing on her flat belly, right above the band of her jeans. The room temperature shot up about a thousand degrees.

"Years ago... You mean two or three?" He unzipped Iris's snowsuit and wriggled her free, happy to have this cute little distraction to keep his hands busy.

Tate's hands dropped to her sides and the stud disappeared. So did her smile. "Why do you do that?"

He had no idea what she was talking about, but he sensed danger. "Do what?"

"Find ways to point out the age difference between us. For the record, I'm twenty-five—so unless your publicist lied, that makes it nine years. And I might have been a big fan of yours when you were competing, but I was never a groupie, if that's something you're worried about. I am curious, though—what's the magic number for you? Two years? Five? Because the only number that mattered to most of the bull riders I ever met was the age of consent."

Miles winced. The age of consent was sixteen in most states. In his early days on the circuit, he'd drawn the line at eighteen to be safe, because some girls developed faster than others and it wasn't always easy to tell. Looking back, he was embarrassed by what had been his biggest concern. He could well imagine what a pretty girl like Tate would have endured.

For the life of him, he could not figure her out. She'd

followed his career, and he could tell she was a big fan, but she didn't act like any of the female fans he'd ever met. She could be flirty, but in a harmless, not to be taken too seriously, way. She said what she thought—which he liked—but not what she *felt*, which disturbed him, because while all hell had not yet broken loose, he suspected it would. Emotionally, she was a landmine.

And she didn't hold him in awe. Why the hell not?

Maybe his shine had worn off for her once he'd retired. Or maybe after his famous face had been damaged. Or maybe since Iris had now entered the picture. At least she hadn't brought up Iris's mother, who was too close to Tate's age for his personal comfort—although age and blond hair were about all the likenesses the two women shared.

"You knew the wrong men," he said lightly, because why not be a hypocrite. He found Tate attractive, but he was at a far different point in his life, and he didn't need her brand of trouble in it. Bringing up her age was a way of reminding himself to keep his hands off. "My limit has more to do with maturity than some random number. And for the record, I have zero interest in teenaged girls," he added, in case it really had to be said.

Tate's frown bent a faint scar that cut through her right eyebrow. "Did you just call me immature?"

"Of course not." Except that was exactly what he'd just done. "I'm reminding myself that I have a lot more life experience under my belt than you do." Which made it sound as if he was attracted to her even though he should know better. Which was true. Which made him feel about as creepy as Santa.

Iris squirmed and stiffened her legs, wanting down. He was fast learning to recognize the signs of an impending temper tantrum. She'd only thrown two so far, but they'd been doozies, and both had involved hunger, so chances were good that she wanted her supper.

A change in subject right now would be more than welcome, as well, because he was putting entirely too much thought into something that shouldn't matter, since he had no intentions of getting involved with Tate. He doubted if she had any intentions of getting involved with him either.

But he couldn't help wondering why not—had he really become so unappealing to women? *Still ninety-five percent pretty. Right?*

He thrust Iris at her. "Here. You can feed her while I heat up the lasagna."

Tate cuddled his fretful daughter, who must have recognized who her real meal ticket was, because she stopped squirming. He got quite a rush from the sight of the two of them together—blond, pretty Tate and the sweet little girl who looked like her proud daddy.

He *liked* Tate. He really did. But the mental bandwidth she consumed wore him out.

They had to pass through the living room on the way to the kitchen. He'd already set the tree up and it was ready for lights. An enormous box of shiny ornaments spilled its insides nearby. Elizabeth O'Connell had insisted he take them because Dallas and Hannah—okay, Dallas—had gone overboard and bought far more than the ranch could possibly use.

Tate stopped and ogled the fat Douglas fir, a purchase inspired by his recent waterfront shopping excursion and the impressive Christmas display. "What is it with Texans? Bigger is not always better."

He slapped a hand to his chest, not about to admit that he'd had to lop two feet off the top to fit it into the room, but happy to roll with her mood swings. "Nobody needs that kind of negativity, ma'am. When it comes to Christmas, bigger is always better."

He got a different kind of rush just thinking about it. Sure, this year would be quieter than he was used to. And homesickness was a real thing. But Iris made it worthwhile. And it would be fun to include Tate, even if she was quirky, combative, and emotionally repressed. Figuring her out was a challenge, and he'd always liked those.

They squeezed past the tree and entered the kitchen, his favorite room in the house, the one he'd renovated first and where he'd spent the most money.

"Wow." She blinked as she surveyed the changes he'd made. "This doesn't look at all the way I remember."

"Glad to hear it. Because it looked pretty dismal."

It had taken him weeks to get rid of the smell of funky

old dog. He'd ripped up the floor, then torn out the wall between the kitchen and dining room, and turned it into one enormous, shared space. He'd installed stainless steel, industrial appliances. The island was industrial-grade stainless steel, too, with a giant butcher block on one end and a bowl of fresh fruit in the middle. Pots and pans hung from the ceiling, within easy reach. He'd added a table for six in front of the window that overlooked the frozen back yard. Right now, because it was night outside, the thick glass reflected the kitchen. He'd positioned Iris's new high chair between the sink and the island so he could keep her entertained while he cooked.

And Miles liked to cook. He liked the preciseness of peeling and cutting and dicing. He liked experimenting with spices and different ingredients. He especially liked presentation, something he'd learned from his mother.

No one needed to know how many hours he'd invested in picking out place mats, utensils, and dishes. Or, for that matter, how much he liked to shop.

He repositioned Iris's chair to the opposite side of the island so that she and Tate wouldn't be in his way, then he got down to business. He grabbed a few jars of baby food from one of the cupboards. He planned to start making her meals fresh once they got past the rodeo, but until then, she was stuck with this slop. To be fair to the manufacturers, she appeared to enjoy it.

Tate knew the feeding drill even better than he did, so he

left her to it and opened the fridge. The home-cooked lasagna he pulled out had crumbled Corizon sausage mixed in with the ground meat and smoked Gouda layered on top. He'd used gluten-free pasta—not to avoid wheat, but because he preferred the firm texture.

He eased the half-empty pan into the oven and adjusted the heat. No warming up leftovers in the microwave for him, not unless he was in a serious hurry, and tonight, that wasn't the case. Tonight was about starting a Christmas tradition with Iris, and hopefully, giving Tate's holiday spirit a boost. What had happened to her twin was tragic, no doubt about it. But, as his pragmatic mom always said, life was for the living.

His mom would never, not in a million years, abandon the remainder of her family if he'd been killed in the arena. She'd be sad, sure. But she didn't play favorites.

Tate accepted a glass of red wine and commented when he didn't pour one for himself.

"If you're worried about driving me home, there's no need for you to take Iris out again when I can catch a ride with Ford," she said, nudging the bottle toward him.

Even though she made sense, since the taproom was only a few minutes away, it didn't sit right to send her home with her brother after he'd asked her out. But this wasn't a date, and he really did have Iris to think of, and it really would be more convenient if Ford came by to pick her up, so he filled a glass for himself, then set to work on putting a salad together. He wasn't much into sugar, so he had no dessert in the house, but he did have fresh rolls from the local bakery.

Tate finished feeding Iris before the lasagna was ready.

"We need to work on your table manners," Miles said to his daughter. She had mashed peas in her hair and a sleepy smile on her custard-smeared face. He got out the plates, napkins, and flatware and left Tate to set the table while he cleaned Iris up and zipped her into pajamas.

Once Iris was dolled up and pretty in pink, the lasagna was out of the oven, and they'd taken their loaded plates to the table, a little Christmas music seemed in order to set the right tone for a tree-trimming party. He could see Tate's heart still wasn't in it and he couldn't have that. He pegged her as someone who'd prefer the classics to pop versions, if her reaction to Gwen was a sign. He'd mounted a flat-screen TV on one kitchen wall and within seconds, Nat King Cole softly sang *"Chestnuts roasting by an open fire..."* into the room while they ate.

Tate had a good appetite. No girlish, *oh, I couldn't possibly eat all of that,* pretense from her and he enjoyed watching her show of appreciation for his cooking.

Iris played on the floor with the new toys he'd bought her—just a few little things to tide her over until Christmas because she needed *something*—but he still didn't have gifts for Sydney and Pax, which made him feel guilty. He didn't want them to think he'd forgotten about them, especially now that he had a child of his own to fuss over. He had two weeks left to get them each something special.

"I take it from the tree and the music that Christmas was a big deal in the Decker family household when you were growing up," Tate said, setting her fork on the edge of her plate.

"And continues to be. Decorating the tree is a huge production."

The tree normally went up the day he arrived home for the holidays. He would have missed the family party by now, which was fine. Let the traditions become about Sydney, Pax, and Iris, not the thirty-four-year-old retired bull-riding baby of the family.

"What was your favorite family Christmas tradition?" he asked Tate.

She hooked a strand of blond hair behind her ear and took a thoughtful sip of her wine. "The Christmas Eve party at the Methodist church."

Interesting. The church she referred to was the First Methodist Memorial, a pretty little building on the outskirts of Grand with lots of stained-glass and rustic white clapboard and mature trees bordering its grounds. It overlooked the Tongue River, not the Yellowstone, which would have been the main thoroughfare in the late 1800s. The banks of the Yellowstone were where St. Joseph's Mission, Grand's older, statelier, founding Catholic church, would already have been well-established by the Irish community.

The woman who'd jingled Santa's bells was a churchgoer… at least once a year. Now he was even more curious about her. "What was so special?"

"Everything." Wistfulness tainted her tone. "Tanner and I loved buying little gifts for the children's party held in the afternoon. Mom baked cookies for it, then fancier treats for the adult party following the midnight service. The pastor's wife, Enid, makes sure the church is decorated from top to bottom, and it's always a candlelit service. Mom used to say it gave her a chance to decompress from the holiday rush and remember what the season is really about."

"My mom says the same thing."

"Yes, well." Tate rose and began clearing the table. "Things change. Mine took up golf so that's what she'll be doing Christmas Eve. And Christmas Day."

Miles had no words for what he thought of her parents. Yes, Tate and Ford were adults, but somehow, he doubted if they were much support for each other. There wasn't a whole lot he could do about Ford. Tate was a different story entirely. Prickly or not, she was going to enjoy Christmas.

He took her plate from her and plunked it on the table, next to his own. "The dishes can wait. That's what a dishwasher's for." He swept Iris off the floor and swung her high. Her chubby legs churned, spinning the pedals on an invisible bicycle. "Let's crank up that music and get down to business. I've got eggnog and a little rum to go with it. It's tree-trimming time."

Tate

"YOU'RE NEW AT this, aren't you? The star goes on last," Tate said to Miles.

He had to be new at it, because getting the star into place was the least of his problems. He held the crowning crystal of glory in his work-roughened hands. It was delicate and shiny and bright—and would add another six inches to a tree that already terrorized the paint on the living room ceiling.

"You think so? And how do you propose we do that?" he asked. "Picture it loaded with ornaments and lights."

They both studied the tree. It took up nearly half the room, and the room wasn't small.

"You're right," Tate said. It killed her to admit it. "In fact, you're never going to get that star mounted. Your tree is obese."

The scar on Miles's cheek crinkled. Humor trickled from his eyes. "Are you body-shaming my tree?"

"I'm questioning your judgment. It looks like Audrey II."

Miles raised his eyebrows. "Audrey had better be a su-permodel."

"Seriously?" Tate couldn't believe it. "It's the carnivorous plant in *Little Shop of Horrors*. Movie? Musical? Performed by just about every drama department in high schools across

North America?" She dropped her voice to the lowest pitch she could reach and belted out, "*Feed me, Seymour. Feed me all night long...* Don't leave Iris alone with it," she finished darkly.

He cracked up, his shoulders quaking with laughter. Iris, who'd fallen asleep on the floor on a blanket, stirred without opening her eyes. Her tiny lips curled into a reflexive smile before relaxing again. The sound of his laughter had Tate smiling, too. The way he energized a room just by being himself was truly astounding. Not much wonder he'd been such a crowd favorite.

And why she still had this huge urge to fangirl all over him—except she had no intentions of ever being one of those women who couldn't leave him alone. She knew the difference and where the line was.

"You played Audrey in your school play, didn't you?" he said when he finally stopped laughing.

"Of course, I did. It was the best part. But we haven't solved the problem of how to get the star on the tree," she pointed out.

Miles rubbed the back of his neck while he studied the problem some more. "The tree is only eight feet tall. If I gave you a boost, you could reach it," he suggested.

Only eight feet... Sure. If she didn't mind getting scratched by all those sharp, prickly needles on the thick clusters of branches. "Why don't I climb the tree, instead?"

He responded with a touch of good-natured sarcasm of

his own. "You'd do that for me?"

"Not in this lifetime, Texas," she said. "But you're welcome to give it a try."

For a second, he looked as if he might be seriously considering it. Then he said, "I have a better idea."

She stood to one side while he took the tree from the stand, lopped another few inches off the top, and tied the star into place with a thin piece of wire. She helped him wrestle the tree upright again, then stepped back to get a good look and prepared to pass judgment.

"It's beautiful," she said. "Still fat, mind you. But more in a majestic kind of way, and less overfed."

"It's as if you're determined to hurt Audrey's feelings," he said. "Ever consider that your friend Maybe isn't the only person around here who's mean?"

"I never said I wasn't mean. But I do like babies a whole lot more than she does."

And she'd missed joking around with someone who had the same sense of humor a lot more than she'd realized. Miles was exactly what she'd needed tonight. He didn't get bent out of shape when she said stupid things, like that idiot remark about the age of consent. She had no idea where that had even come from. If she wanted him to see her as an adult, she should probably behave more like one, but she'd never been good at filtering what came out of her mouth.

"Rockin' Around the Christmas Tree" blared from the kitchen TV. Miles sang along with it as they began stringing the lights. He had a great voice, Tate discovered, surprised there was a personal fact about him that she didn't know. It was a deep, rich, country-style baritone that he dropped into the lower ranges on a few notes for comedic effect, proving she wasn't the only ham in the room.

"*Mistletoe hung where you can see...*" Miles stopped. "That's what's missing," he said, snapping his fingers. "Mistletoe. There's got to be some in here, somewhere."

He dove into the box of decorations and began pulling things out, scattering them with such little regard for organization that Tate's obsessive-compulsive tendencies shuddered in horror.

"Found it!" Miles straightened, triumphant, and held a large cluster of red berries aloft. "Do you know where the tradition of kissing under mistletoe comes from?"

"From ancient state senators who wanted to pretend kissing young girls was okay, so they passed a law saying if they caught one under the mistletoe, she had to kiss them whether she liked it or not?" Tate guessed.

"Interesting take on it, but no," Miles said. "It comes from an old Norse legend. The short version is that the goddess Frigga's son, the god of innocence and light, was killed by an arrow made from a sprig of mistletoe. Frigga declared that from then on, mistletoe would only promote love and peace. Anyone caught standing under it, even mortal enemies, would have to set their weapons down, exchange a kiss of peace, and declare a truce for a day."

"In that case…"

Impulsiveness had always been an issue for Tate. She took the mistletoe from him and held it over his head, then stretched to kiss him before he could dodge out of reach. She'd meant it as a joke. To be funny. And for the first second, it was.

A second later, however, things changed.

Because Miles Decker, even when caught off guard, knew how to kiss.

Chapter Seven

Tate

TATE CLOSED HER eyes and let him take charge. A rope-roughened hand, the texture at odds with the gentleness of its touch, cupped her cheek. A thumb set fire to the bare skin below the ribbing of her cropped sweater. He brushed his lower lip against hers, then followed it up with the tip of his tongue. She curled her fingers into the front of his shirt and went along for the ride.

Which ended right around the eight-second mark. He dropped his hands and put a few inches between them, which was a shame, because her knees were *really* unstable, and if she collapsed at his feet she'd have to lie there and die.

"Those senators had the right idea," he said, rubbing his neck.

"I kissed you," she pointed out, because she never knew when to shut up. If he wanted the credit for it, she should let things alone and give it to him.

"We're back to the Norse, then…" The few inches of space turned into feet. "What's our truce going to be about?"

"We aren't mortal enemies, either."

"True. But a deal is a deal. You don't mess with Frigga. Haven't you ever heard the expression 'sealed with a kiss'?"

He was sounding her out. She heard the question beneath the light banter. She read it in the warm green and gold of his eyes. And she was so, so tempted. This was *Miles Decker*. Any other girl would have her clothes off by now.

Not Tate. She might be a fan, but she wasn't a number. She'd never been one of those girls. She didn't try and fool herself into thinking she was anyone so very different, however. She'd started things with that kiss, and of course he'd have to wonder how far she'd take it.

As tempting as it was though, she couldn't do it. He'd made her feel special all evening and she wanted to hang onto that feeling, at least for tonight. But he didn't get to pretend her age was a problem for him any longer.

She tipped the mistletoe from her hand, returning it to the packing box full of bright ribbons and colorful glass. "How about we get back to work and finish decorating the tree?"

"Do we hang the large ornaments on the bottom and the smaller ones at the top? Or do we shake it up and hang everything random?" he asked.

With that casual question, things returned to normal between them, proving he knew how to take no for an answer—although she doubted that he heard it too often, so maybe he was confused.

"I can't believe your mother let you near the tree. The big ones go on the bottom," she said.

"A truce usually involves compromise, you know. I never would have expected the woman who trimmed Santa's tree to be so averse to shaking things up. But fine. We'll do it your way."

They sipped rum and eggnog and argued over the garland while Elvis dreamed of a white Christmas. The eggnog was thick and sweet, with only a faint hint of rum, because as Miles said, the goal was to stay warm, not get drunk.

Tate hung the last ornament while Miles plugged in the lights. A soft white glow filled the room rather than the brilliance of a midday sun that she'd half-expected, considering the number he'd insisted were needed.

Iris hadn't moved from her spot on the floor. "I should really put her to bed," Miles said, and Tate suffered mixed feelings, because as soon as he did, she'd have no reason to stay.

The thought of heading home to a bleak, cheerless, distinctly unfestive trailer burst her happy bubble. She should put up a tree for Ford, too. A small one. She didn't know where her mother's ornaments were stored, but she could always pick up cheap ones on sale at the mall—although Maybe might have to get them for her, since it would be a while before she'd be welcome again. *Stupid Santa.*

"What are you thinking?" Miles asked.

That his eyes were amazing—green, gold, and brown—

and what a great kisser he was. She was thinking how good his cologne smelled and how much she'd enjoyed everything about this whole evening. She'd always known there was a difference between Miles the public figure—the one whose posters had adorned her bedroom walls—and who he was in real life. She hadn't expected the reality of him to be more perfect, not less.

She plunked her empty glass on a side table. The heavy crystal caught the sparkling lights from the tree. He'd been the perfect distraction, but sooner or later, the evening had to come to an end. No need to wear out her welcome. "That I've had enough rum and eggnog. I should be going."

Miles frowned. "Ford won't be off work for another two hours at least."

"There's no reason for you to have to wait up for him, too. I'll be fine at the taproom."

"I can't let you walk over alone at this time of night, but by the time I get the truck warmed up and Iris in her car seat, we might as well have waited for him here."

"This is Grand, not New York. It's only two blocks and I've walked it plenty of times."

"*I really can't stay...*" Marilyn Maxwell sang out, interrupting whatever Miles might have said next.

"*Baby, it's cold outside,*" Dean Martin crooned in response.

The corner of Miles's mouth lifted, softening the scar's puckered edges. "I think Dean is trying to send you a message."

"Dean should mind his own business." Because she didn't want to go either and Dean wasn't helping.

"How about this? You call me on your cell and talk to me while you walk," Miles suggested, following her to the door.

"What will we talk about?"

His smile broadened. "You never seem to have any trouble with words. I'm sure you'll come up with something."

He'd been so wonderful all evening. So much fun. It bothered her as to what he might think of her hot-and-cold behavior, but tonight hadn't been the right night.

She donned her coat, pulled up the zipper, and struggled for words. "Thank you," she said, feeling all kinds of awkward. "This was the anniversary of my brother's accident. It was a really rough day for me and you made it okay."

"Glad I could help." He reached over and adjusted her scarf. He didn't give trite condolences or ask any questions, somehow understanding that, if she'd wanted to talk about it, she would have done so already. "Call me," he added.

She dug her phone from her pocket and opened the door. Night yawned, most of the neighborhood either already asleep or tucking itself in. A few scattered Christmas lights dotted the street. She waggled the phone at him and threw out a challenge, just for fun and to get things between them back on the right track. "How about you sing to me?"

He drew his own phone from his back pocket and delivered a grin that had Tate's heart hopping. *He is* so *gorgeous.*

"I hope you like Celine Dion's version of 'O Holy Night,'" he said.

"I've heard worse ones."

"And you're about to."

She smiled all the way to the taproom, listening to him hit the highs and lows with amazing precision. *"Behold your king! Before him lowly bend!"* It might not be up to Celine's standards, but even so, it was impressive. Was there nothing this man did not do well?

"Don't forget the party Friday night," he said before they hung up.

Tate

TATE HAD PLENTY of ugly Christmas sweaters in storage somewhere—they'd once been another family tradition, along with church Christmas Eve—but something pretty enough to wear to the party at the Endeavour tomorrow night?

Not in her closet. She picked up her phone and called Maybe.

"I'll be right there," her friend said once she learned of the problem. This wasn't her first rodeo featuring Tate and her poor sense of style.

Tate sprawled, spreadeagled, on the sagging twin bed, and stared at the cheap light fixture on the ceiling while she waited. She hadn't seen much of Miles the past few days. She wasn't sure if he was avoiding her, if he was too busy with rodeo preparations, or a combination of the above. When she did see him, he was as friendly as always. The same as he was with everyone else. She got the message—*don't read too much into the other night.*

Although it was hard not to read anything into that kiss.

A large, meticulously wrapped box on the top shelf of her closet, eating up real estate, caught her eye. It gave her so much guilt whenever she opened the door. Last year, grief had been her excuse. Christmas came and went unacknowledged. This year, she had to do something about it. Saturday morning, after the party, she'd drive to Billings where Dana's parents lived, and leave it up to them to decide as to whether Dana should have it.

A few minutes later, Maybe blew in on a blast of frigid night air, suitcase in tow. The wind snatched the fragile aluminum door from her hand and slammed it against the side of the trailer. She wrestled it into position behind her, flipping the latch so it wouldn't blow open again, then closed the sturdier inner door.

"Where's Ford?" she asked, ditching her knee-high boots on the rubber tray next to the entry and hanging her thick, padded jacket over the rail of a kitchen chair.

"Working."

What Maybe saw in her brother, Tate didn't know. He was handsome, of course. She'd had a steady stream of girlfriends over the years thanks to him. And Tanner, too. But Ford wasn't warm and friendly like Tanner had been, or someone who let people get close, and losing his younger brother—the one the whole family adored—had been especially hard on him.

The real blow, however, had happened a long time ago when the girl he'd dated through high school found a new love after she went off to college. Tate didn't have the heart to tell Maybe she was wasting her time where Ford was concerned. She'd have to figure it out on her own.

Maybe dumped the suitcase's contents onto Tate's bed. Reams of bright-colored fabric spilled across the worn cotton quilt that Tate had been gifted by a grandmother the year she'd turned twelve. Then she stood, with hands pressed to her hips, head tipped to one side, glossy dark hair spilling over a shoulder while she considered the options. She brightened the small bedroom and lifted Tate's spirits through her presence alone.

Tate eyed the bounty. Maybe shared her mother's passion for clothes but was less of an adherent to environmental stewardship. She blew her entire salary on clothes she wore once. Ford—even if interested, which he was not—could never afford her.

Maybe picked up a navy sheath that shimmered in the stark overhead light. The fabric was silky and smooth and didn't look as if it laundered well. "I had to bring what I thought might fit. Mom doesn't have time to make alterations right now."

"That one doesn't look practical," Tate said. "I'll be helping Miles with Iris and she drools." Plus, she could see herself spilling wine down the front. The horror.

Maybe dismissed her concerns with the flap of a hand. "Practical is for my mom and old ladies. I've worn it twice now and likely won't wear it again. Here." She thrust it into Tate's arms. "Try it on."

"What about the black one?" Tate suggested, clutching the navy to her chest, even though she knew from experience that once Maybe took charge, her opinion when it came to clothing was neither desired nor required and carried no weight.

Her friend didn't spare the dress in question a glance. "That one's a last resort. Everyone wears black to evening parties. Now put on the navy."

Tate stripped down to her undershirt and white cotton briefs and Maybe sighed as if giving up. "There's no hope for you."

"Who cares? No one will see my underwear under my dress."

"I'm not worried about anyone seeing it under your dress. I'm worried about who might see it when you take the dress off."

She hadn't told Maybe about tree-decorating with Miles

or the kiss and she wasn't about to bring it up now. "It's not that kind of party."

"It's *always* that kind of party. And it's time you had some fun."

The material slid over Tate's skin like a splash of cool water. The dress was longer on her than on Maybe, which wasn't a problem, because Maybe liked her skirts short. And why shouldn't she? She was five feet and ten inches of head-turning beauty. Good thing Tate loved her too much to be jealous.

She ran her palms down the front of the dress and adjusted the fit. "It's gorgeous."

Maybe frowned. "It looks good on you, but it doesn't scream Christmas."

Tate began to suffer misgivings. Her friend had amazing taste when it came to clothes, but Tate didn't possess the same physical assets. "I'm the babysitter, not part of the décor."

Maybe ignored her and dove into the pile on the bed and emerged with a deep, forest-green dress in what looked like real velvet but most likely was not. "Try this. And lose the undershirt this time."

Tate, who most days preferred comfort to style, stepped into the dress and discovered this one had both, a point in its favor. Beyond that, she had doubts.

The skirt was ruched in the front and back and broke at the knee. The gathered overlay allowed her to move because the fit of the dress on its own never would. The snug bodice was square, with two narrow straps to hold it in place, and a built-in, push-up bra that displayed enough cleavage to stretch Tate's comfort level to unnatural heights. Two detached, full-length sleeves, tight as gloves, covered her arms from shoulder to fingertip, leaving her back bare to the waist.

And she'd though the elf outfit was skimpy.

"It looks amazing on you!" Maybe exclaimed. "When I wear it, I look like a Christmas tree."

That seemed unlikely. But as Tate looked in the full-length mirror on the flimsy bedroom door, she had to agree that, despite the skimpiness, she did look good.

"Now for the shoes. Chastity,"—one of Maybe's five sisters—"said you could wear hers." Maybe dug around in a pocket of the suitcase and pulled out three pairs of high, strappy sandals. "I think these nude ones will work best."

Tate slipped them on and grew three inches taller. Why Chastity, who matched Maybe in height, felt the need to buy heels, was one of life's many mysteries.

"I feel like Cinderella's fairy godmother," Maybe said, dramatically clasping her hands to her chest and fluttering her eyelashes. "If only these were glass slippers."

"You feel like a fairy godmother. I feel like a hooker." Tate already regretted the bodice.

"Only because you're used to sweatshirts and jeans. You should dress like a girl more often."

"The last time I dressed like a girl, Santa got fresh."

Maybe tapped her chin. "No worries there. Santa won't be slipping his hand under the skirt of this dress."

Nobody would. It was far too tight for that. Tate did love it, though. It was beautiful, like every other stitch of clothing her friend owned and was always willing to share. "Thank you. You're the best friend ever."

"And don't you forget it. We still have to do something with your hair, though." Maybe sat on the foot of the saggy twin bed. Her gaze drifted above Tate's head, paused, then settled on the shelf of the open closet. She'd spotted the gift. "*Tate.* You haven't gotten rid of that thing yet?"

"I thought I'd deliver it to Dana's parents this weekend," Tate said, wishing she didn't sound so defensive.

"Why bother? It's not as if Dana's stayed in touch. Let's open it and see what it is, then you can drop it in the mission box at the church or something." Maybe's golden eyes softened as they rested on her. "Dana's moved on." *You should move on, too.*

She was right of course, both in what she said and what went unspoken. But Tate wasn't doing it for Dana. Tying up loose ends for Tanner—doing these little things in his memory—was all she could give him for Christmas, and whatever was in that box, he'd intended for Dana to have it.

"I have to," Tate said. Her friend, who had a twin of her own, should understand why.

"I get it," Maybe said, and Tate didn't doubt that she did. "I also know that Tanner would want you and Dana to be happy. Ford, too," she added. "But he might be a lost cause." She slapped her hands on the bed and bounced the mattress. "You do what you must, but Merry and I are coming over Saturday night. We're bringing decorations and a tree. Ford's probably working, but you are going to be here waiting for us, you're going to tell us how the party went, and the three of us are going to Christmas-up this dump."

It was pointless to argue with Maybe once she'd made up her mind, and Tate discovered she didn't want to, because she couldn't shake the feeling that Christmas was trying to send her a message. She already knew she should put up a tree. It wouldn't be as nice as the one she'd helped decorate with Miles, but it was the thought behind it that counted, and she was lucky to have such good friends.

The party Friday night was going to be fun, too. She smoothed a hand over the plush fabric of the beautiful, borrowed, forest-green dress. She couldn't wait to wear it and see Miles's reaction. There was no harm in flirting with a man who knew how to flirt, too. The trick was in being careful not to read too much into it. To simply have fun.

Because I choose to be happy.

Chapter Eight

Miles

MILES LOVED A good party and the Christmas kickoff at the Endeavour was shaping up to be especially jolly. Thanks went in large part to Dallas Tucker and Elizabeth O'Connell—Dallas for his enthusiasm, and Elizabeth, her good taste.

The Endeavour shopped local. Hannah's taproom provided the beer, Ryan had chosen the wine, and Dan and Jazz came through with mulled cider and rum and eggnog. The Wayside Café had provided pastries and Lou's Pub delivered surprisingly delicate appetizers.

Ryan and Elizabeth had made an executive decision that junior staff and the boys from the group home were to have a separate party because they couldn't possibly police underage drinking. Tonight's party was for vendors and senior staff, and if anyone chose to stay over, the bunkhouses had been opened up for the women and bedrolls provided in the barns for the men.

Miles had moved from his usual bunkhouse and into a

small trailer for the night to make room for the guests. He'd been offered one of the many spare rooms in the ranch house because of Iris, but he'd declined. Overall, she was pretty content, but she was a normal baby, and when out of sorts, everyone within hearing range knew all about it. His bosses didn't need to lose sleep.

She wore her new party dress and was cute as a bug in a rug, as his grandma always said about Sydney and Pax. He couldn't wait to hear what she had to say about her newest great-grandchild. He was less eager to hear what the straight-laced old lady would have to say about him.

He kept a watchful eye on his daughter as the female guests passed her between them, and an impatient eye on the door, waiting for Tate. They'd danced around each other these past few days, pretending that kiss had meant nothing—and her telling him about her brother's anniversary meant even less—and he wasn't sure how long he could keep up his end of it. Tate, he suspected, could go on forever. She seemed big into denial.

She arrived a half hour late. When she took off her coat, she revealed a dress that exposed a great deal more of her than it hid.

Silence settled over the small group of men who'd gravitated around him to pick his brain about his days on the circuit, wanting his opinions on the upcoming season. His jaw slackened, although he managed to keep his mouth closed. Barely.

"Is that *Tate Shannahan*?" someone asked, breaking the spell. He sounded so insultingly incredulous that Miles fought off an urge to punch him for it. Tate was beautiful no matter what she had on.

Tonight, she surpassed beauty. Blond hair spilled over bare shoulders in long, loose, spiral curls. Athletic, not slim, she filled that tight dress in a way that dried out his tongue and made the rest of him sweat. That dress was a message and he hoped it was intended for him. They had the matter of that kiss to resolve.

"Well, well, well. If it isn't Santa's little helper," someone said. He was an older man—Jeff someone-or-other, whose wife stood beside him.

The comment was followed by a smattering of laughter from the guy's male companions and Miles had visions of spending the rest of the night scrubbing blood off the floors. It looked as if Santa's helper could use a little help of her own. He prepared to move in and rescue her—or her unwitting victim. He wasn't sure which at this point.

Neither one, as it turned out. She took the comment in stride. "There's plenty more where that came from, Jeff," she said, sounding friendly enough, but that could be to lull him into a false sense of security before she swooped in for the kill. "Would you like a demonstration?"

"No thanks," Jeff replied. "I like my Christmas presents handled with care."

"Keep talking and your presents will be handling themselves from now on," his wife informed him.

More laughter followed that comment. With the focus off her, Tate's gaze swept the room. It passed over Miles as if they'd never met and settled on Iris. Her lovely face brightened.

He should be pleased that she was more interested in his daughter than him, considering he'd hired her for Iris's benefit, not his, but he was new enough at this fatherhood thing, and aware enough of the scar on his face, to be disconcerted. What if she wasn't into denial, and the dress wasn't a message, and he was delusional?

Now that he was no longer a professional bull rider, his dynamics with women appeared to have changed. A few weeks ago, he hadn't cared. Tate changed all that.

Despite the high heels she wore, Tate sidestepped the people blocking her path with the skillful agility of someone used to taking tight cloverleaf turns on a horse.

Miles loved high heels on a woman. There was something so sexual about the way women moved when they wore them—Tate in particular, because in her case, it was unconscious. It was like her to put on a dress designed to attract attention, then have no idea how much male attention she'd drawn.

He, meanwhile, was very aware and he couldn't say that he liked it. He'd never worried about competition before— in or out of the arena—but Tate was the only unattached woman here and he wasn't about to let her be circled by wolves.

"Excuse me," he said abruptly, his attention on Tate, cutting off one of the rodeo suppliers in mid-sentence, anxious to reach her before some other wolf did.

He cut a direct line through the crowd, focused on his goal. He got to her at the same moment Iris wriggled out of Dan McKillop's mom's grasp, holding her arms out to Tate.

"It's past her bedtime. Even party girls have limits," Tate said to Freda McKillop, explaining Iris's eager defection.

Iris made herself at home on Tate's shoulder and stuck a thumb in her mouth, a sure sign Tate was right, and she'd had enough. She snuggled a fistful of Tate's hair to her cheek like a blond security blanket. The sight of a lovely woman holding his baby with so much contentment filled Miles with all kinds of feels.

"Which is why Elizabeth set up the playpen in their private living room—so I can put her to bed without having to leave the party," he interjected before his thoughts could get carried away. "She's made the rounds of the room, met everyone, and showed off her pretty dress. She can call it a night."

"Speaking of pretty dresses… Yours is beautiful," Freda said to Tate. "Is that one of Cloda's creations?"

"It is," Tate confirmed.

Raiden Strong had drifted up behind her, close enough to join the conversation without butting in. "The dress isn't all that's beautiful. Looking good, Tate. Real good." He smiled at her in a way that seemed harmless enough, but Miles didn't like.

He liked Tate's response even less. "Thank you," she said, a light, pretty pink flushing her cheeks.

Damn. Miles had wanted to be the one who paid her that compliment and put that smile on her lips.

"If you get Iris into her pajamas, I'll come tuck her in," he said to her, even though this was supposed to be her night off and she was a guest. Anything to get her out of Raiden's reach. The other man was too smooth. Too successful. Too attractive to women. All the things Miles used to be, and still was—except the gap between him and the competition had closed.

If Tate objected, no one would know. "I'll tuck her in, too."

She moved off, carrying Iris, her progress slowed whenever someone stopped her to say hello. She'd grown up in Grand, after all. The town wasn't big, and it stood to reason that everyone in it would know her.

"That girl has taken to childcaring like a horse to a bucket of oats," Freda remarked to no one in particular. "Which isn't a real surprise, even if she was wild growing up, all things considered. She mothered that brother of hers as if she were twenty years older than him, not five minutes."

"Iris does seem to like her," Miles said. He was dying to ask questions about Tate but knew better than that. "It's hard to believe she was wild." Which was a complete lie. He had no trouble at all believing Tate had been a handful to raise. He hoped Iris was, too.

"Oh, please." Freda's eye roll and the laughter of the people around her—Raiden included—said they either knew he was lying or thought he was stupid. "The only reason that girl didn't ride bulls herself was because she'd do anything to please her brothers and they drew the line."

Tate riding bulls… That didn't tax his imagination at all. But if she'd given up on the idea because her brothers had protested, then she hadn't wanted it badly enough. It did make him wonder, though. What did Tate want out of life that she'd be willing to fight for? Did she have any idea? Or was she figuring that out?

"Her parents had nothing to say?" Miles decided that question was safe.

Freda sniffed. "Beau and Leslie Shannahan didn't care what those kids did. Still don't. They sold their son's truck and equipment, pocketed the life insurance policy payout, and used the money to move to Florida. You'd think they won the lottery, not lost a son."

"Grief makes people do strange things," someone said. "I'm not defending them. Just pointing out that they've had some hard knocks and aren't all bad. Plus, it's easy to tell other people what they should do with their money when you have lots of your own."

And…

That was Miles's cue to move on, because the conversation was about to get heated. Everyone—including Miles, who was the newcomer here—knew that Freda's son Dan had inherited a sizeable chunk of money along with the ranch, and that he was generous with family.

He moved around the room, from one cluster of guests to another, working his way toward Ryan and Elizabeth's private suite without being too obvious about it. He snagged a sprig of mistletoe from the door of Ryan's office when no one was looking. Elizabeth had likely placed it there as her idea of a joke. It sure wasn't because any of the ranch hands wanted to catch Ryan under it. Frigga's decree or not, he wasn't the kind of man who'd kiss and make peace for a day, with his wife the only possible exception. He dropped the mistletoe into his jacket pocket.

The lights were dimmed when he tiptoed into the O'Connells' private living room where Tate was leaning over the playpen, tucking a blanket around Iris, who was already asleep. Miles never got tired of watching his daughter. He couldn't believe he'd been a part of making something—someone—so amazing.

"Hi," he said softly to Tate, even though from his brief experience, there was little chance of waking up Iris. He'd carry her to the trailer later, and come morning, she'd never know she'd been moved.

Tate straightened. She turned and smiled at him, and his heart did one-armed side pushups. The way she looked at him, as if she were happy to see him—and the way he was now, not as some bull rider she used to admire—pumped him up better than any winning ride ever had. She lit up the same way for Iris, and he imagined her brothers, too, and anyone important to her.

She didn't light up this way for Raiden Strong. He would have noticed.

"Hi," Tate whispered back. "She's asleep."

"I see that."

He gazed down at his daughter. He had to make up his mind. He could pursue Tate. He felt confident she'd be receptive. But if he got involved with her, and she wasn't ready for anything serious, where did that leave him? Because he was ready for more. He'd been feeling that way already, which explained why he'd been skittering around the decision to head to Texas for Christmas even before Iris's arrival, which had altered the stakes. His decisions now affected her, too.

Tate tapped his hand, which squeezed the playpen's rail in a white-knuckled death grip. "You seem pretty tense," she said. "If you're worried about leaving Iris alone in a strange place, I don't mind staying with her while you go back to the party."

"Or," Miles countered, testing the waters, "I could take Iris home while you stay and enjoy yourself. You look beautiful and there's no reason for that dress to go to waste."

Here's where most women would say, *I wore the dress just for you.*

Not Tate.

"I'm only here because you invited me. Nobody said anything about me having to enjoy myself, too."

This was why he found her so entertaining. Even her flirting was honest. Piecing together what she was being honest about was the challenge.

Challenge accepted. "Have you ever considered not completing a whole thought out loud? Because that statement would have worked best if you'd stopped after, 'I'm only here because you invited me.'"

"If you want me to enjoy myself, you're going to have to put some serious effort into making it happen," she replied.

Effort wasn't the word he would have chosen, although it intrigued him. "I see how this works. You expect me to do the heavy lifting."

Tate spun around, a trace of vanilla swirling with her as she showed off her dress. "I did the prep work. If I have to do the heavy lifting myself, too, then I don't need you."

The thought of Tate doing her own heavy lifting scattered his brain in a hundred directions. "You have a point. How much heavy lifting are we talking about, She-Ra?"

"How much enjoyment do you plan on me having?" she countered, her eyes as saucy as her smile.

And here was where the script diverged yet again. While he greatly enjoyed pleasuring women, most women talked about how much pleasure they planned to give him. He'd once had a woman lick his belt buckle on the dance floor of a crowded bar. The actual sex act had occurred in the alley behind it, where she'd done things to him that he'd never heard of before, and all it had cost him was a selfie.

They'd both been so stupid and young.

He didn't want stupid and young anymore. Tate might be young, which made him justifiably nervous, but he didn't believe she'd ever been that kind of stupid. Sex would mean more to her than a chance to lick a retired bull rider's buckle or give birth to a paycheck.

He wanted to know how serious she was.

"I think," he said, "that I'm more into showing, not telling. We can leave through the back door. We'll put Iris in her crib and hope she sleeps through the night. Then I plan to show you. Unless you'd rather stay for the party. Or do your own heavy lifting?"

Tate eased into his arms. The high heels put them at eye level. She kissed him, slowly and sweetly, no mistletoe—which remained in his pocket—required.

"While having options is nice, I've never been much into parties. There are also instances where doing my own heavy lifting is overrated. This," she said, her lips beginning a slow walk across his cheek and down the side of his throat as she spoke, "is one of them."

Good enough for him. "I'll grab our coats."

Chapter Nine

Tate

TATE TOOK OFF her heels and hung her coat over the arm of a tattered black leather sofa in the front room, then sat down to wait while Miles put Iris, still sound asleep, in her crib. While sleeping with her boss might not be one of Tate's smarter moves, what was the worst that could happen? She'd get fired?

Because she'd already gotten fired from a job as an elf. It would take a lot to top that.

He joined her on the sofa before she could compile a complete list.

It was all kinds of wrong for a man who'd earned his money riding bulls to look so good in a suit, but he pulled it off with the same confidence he did everything else. Flutters tickled her chest but raised no alarms. Excitement, it turned out, felt a whole lot like panic, but she wasn't going to have any regrets. She'd consider this her Christmas gift to herself.

He stretched both arms over his head, let out a loud, exaggerated yawn, then dropped one around her shoulders as if he were a fourteen-year-old trying to cop a feel on his first date. "Hey, baby. Come here often?"

Not often enough. Panic wasn't a concern, but nervousness was. Her heart pounded like crazy, and she prayed her palms wouldn't sweat. She hadn't had sex in forever and her lack of practice was starting to show. She discarded the role of high school cheerleader who put out for the whole team, and she'd never pull off hot teacher, so she withdrew a handful of condoms from her coat pocket and went for a brisk, business transaction.

"Don't read too much into why I have these with me. Maybe insisted I come prepared," she said, tumbling the shiny foil packets into his hand.

Miles looked at them as if he'd never seen a condom before. Then, he looked at Tate. One eyebrow shot up. "Are we skipping foreplay?"

Tate sighed. "You're a talker, aren't you?"

"A talker?"

"Someone who feels the need to discuss every move. Offering up play-by-plays. '*Ooh, baby. Tell me you like this. Come for me, baby.*' It stems from a man's insecurities around his performance."

Miles's eyes narrowed. "I have never in my life felt insecure about any performance of mine."

"Oh, I'm not talking about riding a bull," she said, enjoying his pretense of outrage, and the fact he was playing along. Her heart rate didn't slow down, but excitement could now take some of the credit.

"Neither am I."

"Great. Glad we've gotten the issue of talk during fore-play out of the way. Not a fan."

Miles rubbed the roughened side of his face. "I'm pretty sure I'm not the one with performance anxiety right now."

"You could be right," Tate conceded. "You're Miles Decker, after all. I've got a long string of women to compete with. I'd like to score in the top ten percent."

Audacious fingers tiptoed closer to her breast. She pretended not to notice and snuggled deeper under his arm. "You do understand that you won't be scored on your performance alone, right?" he said. "I own fifty percent of the ride."

"Excellent observation." She patted his thigh. The *muscle*... Every one of her own clenched in response, and her tongue dried a little, but she didn't plan to give in too quickly. There'd be nothing memorable about her in that. "What's your ranking, cowboy, so I'll know what my handicap is and how much heavy lifting is expected of me?"

Miles, good sport that he was, pretended to give it some thought. "I'm usually a perfect score, so you pretty much just have to sit tight."

"And hang on for eight seconds," Tate said, nodding, determined to push his man buttons so she wasn't at a complete disadvantage. "I can do that."

"Eight whole seconds... That's it. Foreplay is over."

"Finally. I was beginning to think you were all talk and no action. And that your reputation with women was probably pumped up by your publicist."

"I call for a truce." Miles reached into his jacket pocket and pulled out a sprig of mistletoe that was slightly the worse for wear. He held it over her head and leaned in for a kiss that said he was done fooling around.

It was time to come clean. She plucked at his shirt front and stared at his chin. "I might be a little bit nervous."

"I would never have guessed." He tossed the mistletoe aside. "How about you close your eyes, relax, and let me take care of that heavy lifting you're so concerned about for you? See if I can take the edge off your nervousness, too?"

"You can try. But since you're the one making me nervous, I'm curious as to how you plan to pull this off."

Closing her eyes was easy enough, but relaxing was out of the question. She felt him pause. His fingers brushed against the base of her throat with the lightest of touches before he withdrew them.

"Nervousness is no problem," he said. "If you're having second thoughts, however... That one's the deal breaker."

She opened her eyes and smiled into his. Flecks of dark gold floated like daisies against a field of deep green. She closed hers again and settled more comfortably into the sofa's saggy embrace. "I'm not having second thoughts. I'm not nervous about the sex part. You're the one with the reputation to live up to. I expect to be wowed, but what if I'm disappointed? How do I tell you? I don't want to damage your ego, and it's stressing me out."

His deep chuckle reflected the confidence that made him so famous and such a crowd favorite.

"Thanks to Maybe we have plenty of condoms. I can take my time getting it right." His tongue found a sensitive spot under her ear that she hadn't known she possessed. A warm flush spread across her skin. "Keep your eyes closed until I say you can open them," he said. "No talking. Unless I try something you don't like or aren't comfortable with, of course, in which case, speak up."

His fingers played the length of her collarbone, inching lower, trailing toward the low-cut bodice of her dress. The tip of one finger traced the curved line where fabric met skin, and she sucked in a breath as he tugged the fabric aside. Cool air trickled over one exposed breast. He cupped his palm underneath it and brushed his thumb over her nipple.

He drew the nipple into his mouth, and the sensations he created with his tongue made it impossible for her to remain still. He unzipped the seam on the side of her dress and slid the bodice down to her waist. The tight skirt had hiked up her thighs. Her legs were bare—she didn't own pantyhose and couldn't be bothered buying any—but thankfully, she'd taken Maybe's advice and invested in pretty underwear. Miles knelt on the floor between her thighs and wriggled his hands under her skirt. He hooked his thumbs in the elastic straps that held her panties in place before tugging them down and easing them off—first freeing one foot, then the other—exposing parts of her that rarely saw light. He lifted her leg and ran his hand from her ankle to high on the inside of her thigh. He propped her ankle on his shoulder and hiked her skirt higher. His lips replaced his hand on her thigh, then his tongue. She kept her eyes closed, the second part of the bargain, but thankfully, he hadn't said anything about keeping her hands to herself. She fisted her hands in his hair, urging him forward, silently pleading for more. He gladly obliged. He held her hips steady while his tongue licked the length of her cleft, then explored deeper. She braced her heel on his shoulder, arching her back, and let out a long, soft sigh of pleasure and began to suspect that he was trying his hardest to get her to talk after telling her to remain silent.

Fine. If the goal was to torture each other, she had a reputation of her own to live up to. She fumbled for his fly and unfastened his trousers. He tumbled into her hand, thick and hard, and she touched the tip with her thumb. A grating sound rumbled deep in his throat.

That was more like it.

"Hang on, sweetheart," he said. "We're about to change places."

Seconds later, she straddled his thighs. Her dress bunched around her hips and the bodice flapped to her waist. The sleeves had slid down her arms. Her panties were gone. The only thing preventing full contact between them was a few inches of space. She rested her hands on his shoulders and her knees on the sofa to steady herself. She heard the crinkle of aluminum foil as he reached for a condom packet.

"Not yet," she said. She shifted her weight so that she sat on his knees, then took his erection in hand, and bent her head to lick the beckoning tip. She traced her tongue around the rim of his crown, tasting sweet, salty male. She heard the hiss as he sucked in a deep breath of air. Felt the rise and fall of his chest. She lifted her head and planted a kiss on his mouth, while moving her fingers, wrapped around him, up and down, squeezing ever so gently.

Miles tore open the packet and pressed the condom into her hand. "Open your eyes. I want you to look at me."

She opened them. He was watching her with slumbrous, heavy-lidded desire in his own. His excitement lifted her own to new levels. She rolled the condom in place, fumbling a little, then got to her knees and guided his erection into position. The heavy tip nudged her opening, and she bit her lip, trying to maintain control when in reality she was so desperate for him that she ached.

"Look at me," Miles said again. He held her gaze with his, slowly edging inside her, inch by magnificent inch, until they were joined so completely, she couldn't breathe for the pleasure of it. She wriggled her hips, enjoying the feel of him, the way the movement made him moan. "You're killing me."

"Can I talk now?" she asked.

"I'm not sure I could stop you. My brain's engaged elsewhere." The words came out heavy with effort.

Tate lifted her hips, loving the feel of him as he slid in and out. "That's what I want," she said, barely recognizing her own voice. "Just like that."

He picked up on the rhythm she set. She placed her hands over his, gripping his wrists. Heat rose in her belly and sparked a rippling reaction that had small, tight muscles clenching in joyful expectation. Sensing her orgasm building, he thrust harder and deeper until they were both breathing heavily, and further speech was impossible.

Pinpricks of light exploded inside her head as her orgasm erupted and pleasure consumed her. Miles stiffened. She heard him cry out past the roar in her ears. One of them muttered, *oh, God*, and she suspected it might have been her.

The intensity ebbed and she went limp in his arms, her cheek pressed against his throat as they rode the last waves together, with him pulsing and throbbing inside her. She couldn't move and had no desire to do so.

The soft, idle stroke of his fingers against her cheek brought her back to the moment. They hadn't even fully undressed. His shirt hung, half-unbuttoned, and his trousers flapped wide at the zipper. Her dress was a sorry mess at her waist. The detachable sleeves bunched around her elbows.

Miles combed his fingers through her hair, carefully smoothing out tangles. "Now that we're well past the no-talk-during-foreplay stage, am I allowed to ask if it was as good for you as it was for me?"

"It was okay. I'd give it a seven or eight." More like an eleven. But his ego was healthy enough. Why overinflate it?

"Tough crowd."

He tumbled her to the sofa and disposed of the condom. Then he stooped, and before she deciphered what he had planned, she found herself draped over his shoulder like a sack of buckwheat. He patted her bare bottom, then left his hand on her left butt cheek, his broad palm spreading heat and ideas.

"That was round one. Rounds two and three will take place in the bedroom. You have an item of jewelry attached to your belly that I've been curious about. And when we're finally done putting all your condoms to the test, you're going to be bone-tired and so satisfied, you'll sleep until Christmas."

Chapter Ten

Miles

A SOLID KNOCK on the exterior door woke Miles from a deep sleep. He had no urge to move to find out who it might be. If it was an emergency, they'd knock harder and there would be shouting.

The second knock came again with more momentum behind it. Miles burrowed his face into Tate's hair, breathing deep. Still no shouting. Until then, he was staying right where he was.

"Miles? You in there?"

Miles bolted upright. That sounded a lot like his dad. But it couldn't be. His dad was in Texas.

Now he had to investigate because whoever it was, they were a heartbeat away from waking up Iris and Tate, and they'd both had a late night. His groin tightened a notch at thoughts of the reasons for Tate's. If that wasn't his dad, they'd better have a good reason for the early morning disturbance.

He pulled on the dress pants he'd somehow kicked under

the bed, not wasting precious seconds on finding his shirt. The trailer door wasn't locked, and if it was his dad outside—which the knot in his stomach foreshadowed—then a closed door wouldn't stop him.

He opened the door to find his father impatiently stamping his feet to stay warm against a cold winter wind. Even better—or worse, all things considered—his mom was here, too.

They all stared at each other.

His father ran out of patience first. "Aren't you going to let us in? We had a long drive and it's damned cold out here."

"You drove all the way from Laredo?"

"We drove from the airport Hilton in Billings." His dad's terse tone added, *idiot.*

But all Miles could think of was Iris asleep in one bedroom and a naked Tate in the other. He wasn't sure which girl was going to be harder to explain, but there was no doubt he'd have to explain both, and he had to buy himself a few extra minutes to determine how to best go about it. His parents looked pleasant enough, but when it came to ferreting out truth from their children, Vincent and Helen Decker formed a formidable pair—a no-holds-barred, parental tag team of pro heavyweight champions.

Iris, of course, took that moment to decide to wake up. Normally, she played in her crib for a bit. This morning, after a late night, she was out of sorts, and judging by the impressive strength of her lungs, she was hungry.

His parents, still on the stoop, froze—and not from the cold, which admittedly, was fierce, even by Montana standards.

His mother blinked. "Do I hear a *baby*?"

"I…" Miles's voice died away, because yes, that was a baby she heard. No mistake about that.

And because things weren't bad enough yet, Tate launched herself out of the bedroom in response to Iris's cries. She wore his shirt and not a stitch of anything else, which was going to be really awkward for him to explain—although his parents weren't stupid, so not as much explanation would be required on that front.

Tate saw they had company, and in typical Tate style, carried on as if running around half naked was nothing unusual for her. She disappeared into Iris's room with his shirttail flashing behind her.

His mother pushed him aside and hustled into the trailer, his dad hot on her heels.

His dad closed the door with ominous care. "Did we come at a bad time?" The glare in his eyes warned his calm tone was a complete lie.

"I think we both know the answer to that," Miles replied, because while bull riding had never made him brave enough to smart-mouth his father, apparently hanging with a woman who could make Santa cry did.

The bravado didn't last long. Not once his mother entered the ring. "I hope you used protection," she said.

"Jesus, Mom." Miles closed his eyes. He'd never be able to have sex again if he discussed condoms with her.

"Don't swear at your mother. What the hell is wrong with you, boy?" his dad barked.

Tate reappeared, all bare legs and sleep-tousled hair, but at least with his shirt all the way buttoned this time. She carried Iris, who was not at her best. Her nose ran from crying, she had something crusty stuck in her hair, and she'd worked one chubby leg free of her sleepers. She rubbed her damp face, and as Tate passed her over to him, she transferred her runny nose goo to his shoulder. Then she saw strangers, decided this was a great chance to play shy, and pressed her face into his neck.

"Excuse me," Tate said politely, then disappeared before Miles could introduce her, which was just as well, because his parents were focused on the baby and not paying a lick of attention to anything else.

"This isn't what it looks like," he said, since no one was talking, even though yes, it was exactly how it appeared.

"Why don't you tell us what you think it looks like and we'll see if we're all on the same page?" his mother suggested, not lifting her eyes from the sniffling bundle he held.

Why not tell them the truth and get that out of the way? This couldn't get any worse. "It looks like I got a girl pregnant, she decided she didn't want to be a mother, and a week ago, she dropped a daughter on me. This is Iris, by the way.

She's eight months old. Then, I had to hire a babysitter to look after her. That would be Tate," he added, gesturing with his free hand toward the bedroom, in case they couldn't make the connection themselves. "The ranch had their annual Christmas party last night, and it ended late, so Tate slept over."

"Jesus," his dad said. "I guess that answers the question about protection."

"What are you doing here?" Miles asked, hoping to redirect the conversation, but his parents weren't having that.

"We came for the rodeo, and to take you home for Christmas after," his mom said. "But I see you have your hands full." She began playing peekaboo with Iris, who was about as shy as a hot-tempered bull. His mom quickly caught on and held out her hands. "Give her to me."

"You took a paternity test, right?" his dad said while Miles made the transfer.

His mother glared over Iris's head at his dad, which gave Miles hope she could be swayed to his side. "I think I can recognize my own grandchild."

"If that's true, you're going to be busy," his dad growled. "The boy's likely left a trail of them from Texas to Maine."

Tate reemerged, this time wearing the dress from the previous night. It was wrinkled and the sleeves were uneven, but she looked breathtaking all the same. She squeezed past Miles in her trippy high heels and grabbed her coat from the arm of the sofa in the front room. Everyone watched in silence from the cramped kitchen. Apparently, they all planned to pretend they didn't see the pair of panties on the floor under the flat-screen TV.

She stopped on her way out to give Miles a quick kiss on his scarred cheek.

"I'll pick up more condoms before work Monday morning," she said. "We're all out."

Then she was gone, leaving him on his own to deal with two irate parents and a fussy baby who chose that moment to remember how hungry she was.

Tate

IF TEENAGED TATE had once dreamed of meeting Miles's parents—which she hadn't—she would not have envisioned it unfolding this way.

I had to hire a babysitter... That would be Tate.

Her face burned as she got in her car while the rest of her shivered as she waited for the engine to warm up. So much for wanting to be different than the rest of Miles Decker's fans. She should have kept quiet about the condoms, but she couldn't stand the thought of his parents believing she'd try to thrust another unwanted pregnancy on him. Her babysitter dignity might be damaged, but her pride was intact.

Since her day hadn't gotten off to a great start, and she

didn't plan to sit around dwelling on it because no good could come from that, she might as well take Dana's gift to Billings. Four hours in the car—two there and two back—were what her dignity needed to work out the dents.

She flicked off her phone in case Maybe was too impatient for an update on the party to wait. Hopefully, by the time the sisters showed up to decorate the tree Ford had provided, Tate's sense of humor would have returned. Something about this had to be funny.

Forty-five minutes later, after stopping to change her clothes and pick up the gift, she was on her way to Billings. Two hours after that, and after a couple of wrong turns as she entered the city, she found Dana's parents' house.

The Barretts lived in an older subdivision, in a plain, split-entry home on a lot surrounded by trees and with a dry creek bed that cut past its backyard.

Dana was a big part of why Tate no longer raced. They'd been casual friends up until Dana began dating Tanner. He'd had lots of girlfriends before, but he'd been serious about Dana, and for the first time in her life, Tate had felt so excluded, and she hadn't tried very hard to maintain the friendship. After the accident, the two women could barely look at each other.

She got the gift from the back seat. It was about the size of a breadbox and felt weirdly heavy, as if it had been weighted with something, which it probably had. Tanner loved giving impractical, but meaningful, gifts. She'd once gotten a sword and a scabbard to attach to her saddle. They'd been watching a fantasy series on TV, and she'd expressed an interest in the weaponry used. Hopefully, if Dana's parents decided to give the gift to her, she'd get some pleasure from it.

When Dana herself opened the door, the speech Tate had carefully prepared for her parents departed. Wordlessly, she thrust the box into the other woman's hands.

"What's this?" Dana asked, holding the gift cautiously, as if it might explode any second.

"I found it. With Tanner's things." *A year ago...* Tate managed to stop babbling before blurting out that last part. It wasn't something Dana needed to hear and wouldn't do much for their already strained relationship. "He'd want you to have it."

Dana's cautious reserve thawed. She was a pretty brunette with midnight-blue eyes, thick black lashes, and skin the color of heavy cream laced with vanilla. Tanner had talked about her for days before working up the nerve to ask her out, to the point where Tate had offered to ask her out for him if he was going to be such a sissy about it.

"Come in and open it with me," Dana said. "I'm sure we'll both get a good laugh out of whatever this is."

The tension trickled out of Tate's neck and shoulders. The invitation was generous considering they hadn't spoken to each other since the day of the funeral, or so much as made eye contact, even though Tate hadn't quit the circuit

PARLA ALTENBURG

for another few months.

The Barrett home was warm and cozy and borderline gaudy with Christmas decorations—all the things her own home used to be at this time of year. Dana's mother was in the kitchen, baking cookies. The smell of molasses and ginger teased the tip of Tate's tongue. She stopped long enough to say hello to Mrs. Barrett before Dana led her to the adjoining dining room and offered her a chair.

"I hope it's not something inappropriate for his sister to see," Dana said, caution coating her words, making it more of a warning than a joke.

Tate couldn't imagine anything more inappropriate than what Miles's parents had seen just that morning. "Don't worry. If it is, I'll survive."

Dana opened the box. Inside was another box, with a note on top. She didn't read the note out loud, but her smile turned wistful, and she set it aside, face down on the polished table.

Her smile slowly flattened, like a balloon with a slow leak, as she worked her way through a series of boxes and notes until she got to the final one—a small velvet jeweler's box.

A huge knot of dread formed in Tate's stomach. She should have taken Maybe's advice and opened it first.

Dana didn't open the box. Instead, she took Tate's hand and pressed it gently into her palm. "You keep it. Or return it. Pawn it, or something. I know what it is, and I can't

142

accept it."

Tate tightened her fingers around the soft velvet. "Why not?"

"Because I would have said no."

Her words were a shock. Tate would have sworn they'd been happy together. Tanner had been crazy for Dana and Tate had been so jealous of them. *Please don't let me be the reason.*

Dana began stuffing wrapping paper and packaging into the first, largest box, avoiding Tate's eyes. "Being involved with a bull rider wasn't for me. I was going to break up with him after that last ride."

"I see."

There wasn't much more Tate could say. Guilt turned her chest into a huge block of ice and numbed her hands and lips. Tanner had known. That was why he'd wanted to quit. And Tate, because she could never leave things alone, had insisted he ride.

She dropped the jeweler's box into her purse. She accepted one of Mrs. Barrett's fresh cookies but declined an offer of coffee or tea. She managed a few moments of small talk before escaping to her car.

The return drive to Grand was a blur.

She wasn't ready to go home. Maybe and Meredith would arrive in a few hours to help put up a stupid tree and she was not in the mood.

On a whim, she headed for the small Methodist church.

Pastor Harm Addams—whose first name meant *warrior*, or so he claimed—was an old friend of the Shannahan family. His children had gone to school with Tate and her brothers.

He'd baptized them. He'd officiated at Tanner's funeral and laid him to rest in the cemetery out back. He'd helped walk Tate through the worst of her grief when the Shannahans had nothing left in them to spare for each other. He'd been the one to suggest she might get some comfort from doing something meaningful in Tanner's memory for Christmas.

He'd called that one wrong. As of today, her Christmas spirit was officially dead.

I choose to be happy…

No, Tate, your dead brother is not sending you secret Christmas messages. Grow up. You heard what you wanted to, that's all. Same as always.

How could she ever be happy when she'd ruined any chance at happiness for Tanner and Dana?

Pastor Harm's car wasn't in the small parking lot, but she knew the church would be open, so she slowed down and turned in. She'd sit for a few moments. She'd soak up some of the peacefulness the pretty little church offered. She'd pull herself together.

Then she'd go home, pretend everything was fine—for Ford's sake if not her own—and she'd help Maybe and Meredith decorate the damned tree.

Chapter Eleven

Miles

AFTER A BREAKFAST of pancakes and sausage in the ranch cookhouse alongside a few straggling guests and ranch hands, Miles's parents followed him in their rental to his house in Grand.

Tate's car wasn't home, he noted on the drive past. He'd tried to call her, but it went straight to voicemail, and he didn't dare leave her a message. What would he say? *Make sure you buy extra-large?*

"The tree is lovely," his mother said after he'd given her a quick tour of his house. "And the kitchen is beautiful. But that coatrack has got to go."

She put Iris down for a nap while he and his dad took a walk around the block. He could tell his dad had a lot left to say and the best way to get past this whole morning was to let him get it out of his system.

Miles shoved his gloved hands in his coat pockets and hunkered his chin in his collar. The frigid wind spinning off the mountains held the promise of snow, but the blue, cloudless sky called it a liar. He hadn't gotten used to the cold, but it was on his agenda.

Miles's three-bedroom bungalow was one of the larger homes on the street. Very few houses were more than one story, and the ones that were, tended to have only one or two bedrooms. No historic homes in this section of town, on the outskirts of Grand. The dwellings here had cropped up around the old dairy, now the taproom. He nodded to the neighbors who were also out for a stroll, also enjoying the sunshine, and took note of the babies bundled in strollers as potential playmates for Iris.

"You don't need to bunk down with every blond piece of tail who throws herself at you, you know," his dad started in, proving Tate wasn't the only one who believed in the straightforward approach.

They'd had this conversation before though, and enough was enough. Miles loved his parents, but he was thirty-four, not fourteen, and no longer answered to them. They'd barged in on him unannounced. If they didn't like what they found, that was on them for not calling ahead.

"Hold it right there," he said. "Tate's no piece of tail and she didn't throw herself at me."

His dad's whole attitude changed. He went from antagonizing to paternal in the blink of an eye, as if he'd been handing out a life lesson that Miles was too slow to pick up on.

"No? Then what is she?" his dad probed. "Exactly how

did your babysitter—which is how you described her to us—wind up in your bed?"

Suddenly, Miles saw his mistake and why Tate might be mad. He'd downplayed her importance to him. He'd given the impression she wasn't worth introducing to his parents. It was doubly unfortunate that his dad had to point it out to him, because he should have figured it out on his own.

"I don't know what she is yet," he admitted. "The relationship is pretty new." A little over a week old, in fact. He prayed his dad didn't piece that together. "But she's special."

"She looks young." His dad wasn't being judgmental, simply stating the obvious.

"That's part of the problem," Miles said. "She's twenty-five."

"Twenty-five's not all that young."

"Depends on how you look at it. I've had my shot at a career. She's still finding her path." Babysitting and a brief stint as an elf… Those weren't careers. She didn't know what she wanted in life. And Miles didn't want to stand in her way while she found out.

"She's not ready for a ready-made family?" his dad guessed.

"I have no idea if she is, or she isn't. Like I said—the relationship's new."

"I get it. It's too soon to talk to her about it." His dad draped an arm around Miles's shoulders and rubbed his knuckles into Miles's hair, something Miles had always hated when he was a kid but now found he liked. "If you care about her, maybe you should do some damage control. You could start off by giving her a proper introduction to your parents. You aren't off the hook with us either, by the way— wait until your mother gets past the excitement of a new grandbaby and realizes she wasn't the first to find out."

One more conversation to look forward to.

"Welcome to the club," Miles said. "I wasn't the first to find out either."

Miles

MILES DEEMED IT safe to leave his parents in charge of his daughter so they could bond, since right now, they were a lot happier with her than with him.

It was Tate's mood he was more worried about. He was on his way to the ranch on the pretext that he had work to do, just so he could see if she was home and ignoring his calls, when he spotted her car at the Methodist church.

He parked next to it and got out.

The little church, with its stained-glass windows and white clapboard, had to be the prettiest in Montana. He'd been curious about it and its history ever since learning Tate had a soft spot for it.

He found her inside, huddled in the far end of a pew

next to the wall, all alone and looking miserable, which made him feel guilty as hell. No, he hadn't handled this morning at all well, as his dad had pointed out.

The church was as pretty on the inside as he'd expected, especially with the tree at the front of the sanctuary and the colored lights from the stained-glass windows streaming around it.

The wooden floor creaked under his weight, although the faded runner between the pews that led to the pulpit deadened his footsteps. He eased onto the wooden plank seat and shuffled across until his hip connected with hers. He dropped an arm around her shoulders, encouraged when she didn't push him away. The best thing about her was that she didn't play games. On the flip side, she was terrible at expressing her feelings. They generally exploded in ways that made Santa flinch.

"Want to talk about this morning?" he asked.

"In a church? What are you, a heathen?"

This was the Tate he'd come to admire. "Alrighty, then. Want to hear how my dad read me the riot act and told me to grow up and act like a man?"

"Maybe some other time."

The possibility struck him that he might not be the most important thing going on in her life. "Then may I ask why you're sitting all alone in a church?"

"It's peaceful in here. I drove to Billings this morning."

He didn't see the connection. "I've been to Billings. It

isn't that bad. You didn't knock over a liquor store, did you?"

"Worse. I killed somebody."

She said it so seriously that he had a moment of gut-pinching fear. He couldn't see her deliberately murdering anyone, but considering her track record, accidental homicide wasn't a stretch. "This, I've got to hear."

"I wanted to do something for Tanner for Christmas. He'd bought his girlfriend a present last year, and it's been sitting in this big box in my closet. I thought I'd give it to her for him. Something for her to remember him by." Tate pulled a small velvet box from her purse and showed it to Miles. "I had no idea this was what it was. It didn't go over especially well. It turns out she'd planned to break up with him." She returned the box to her purse. "I probably should have baked her cookies or something."

Miles was in Tate's corner on this one. Dana could have said thank you for the kind thought and left it at that. She didn't have to dump more grief on Tate.

He made a mental note to never propose to her on a special occasion. "Let's get to the dead body," he said. "I take it you killed her for being ungrateful. Do I need to find us a shovel?"

"It's too late for that." Tate laced her fingers together and rested her hands in her lap. "The morning he died, Tanner told me he was done with bull riding and planned to withdraw from his event. I reminded him that our parents had loaned him a lot of money to get started, that he'd had a lousy season, and the prize money was good."

Poor Tate. What an unfortunate memory to live with.

"And because of that you think it's *your* fault he was killed? Sweetheart, let me explain something to you. In those few seconds before the chute opens, a rider has decisions to make—does it feel right? Is your head in the right place? Is this your ride? There are plenty of eyes on you, checking to make sure you're okay. They're checking the bull, too, to see what kind of temper he's in. No one wants to see a rider get hurt."

"Tanner only got into the sport because of me."

"I find that hard to believe." Freda McKillop had said Tate was the one who'd wanted to ride, but that didn't mean Tanner had no interest in it. "No one gets on a bull if they don't enjoy the thrill of the ride."

"It's true. I couldn't find anyone willing to train me, especially after Ford stuck his nose in, so Tanner offered to give it a try if I switched to barrel racing instead."

And as a result, neither one of them had ended up participating in a sport they'd loved, meaning while they'd both been above average, neither had shone. It also explained why she'd walked away from barrel racing so easily—and why her brother had been willing to quit bull riding for a woman.

Miles couldn't have done it. Not in his twenties and not for that reason. But he was glad that her brother had stepped in to divert her, because even though he had nothing against women riders, they had a far tougher go of it in competition than men.

"I don't believe your brother stuck with riding as a favor to you," he said. "I got to the top of the sport because I wanted it so bad, I couldn't imagine not doing whatever it took to get me there. I worked hard and I paid attention. And once I got there, I worked even harder, and paid more attention, because there's always someone younger and hungrier right on your heels. Your brother had a respectable amount of success, meaning he'd expended some effort on the sport, too. But there reaches a point where either your mind or your body can't take those eight seconds anymore. If you're paying proper attention, you see it coming. Trust me, Tanner didn't wake up one morning and make a sudden decision. He would have been thinking about it."

If he'd made a snap decision not to ride on that day, then his girlfriend was more likely behind it—except Miles saw no reason to say so and cause further discord between the two women. It was pure conjecture and too late for that.

"I should have listened to Maybe and not taken that gift to Billings," Tate said. "My only talent seems to be an ability to take any situation and make it worse."

"Your talent is blameless. There was nothing you could do to make this situation worse. Or better, for that matter. And I have got to meet this Maybe, by the way. She sounds like she has more than meanness and a great sense of fashion going for her."

Now that they'd talked through why Tate was sitting in church all alone, she finally remembered she was angry with him. The irritated side-eye she gave him confirmed it—as if there'd been any doubt.

"I'm not introducing you to my friends," she said.

"Why not? I'm introducing you to my parents. They're anxious to meet you." He kissed the top of her head. "I'm sorry about this morning. I handled it poorly, as my dad was happy to tell me."

"Your parents want to meet me?"

"They do. And I want you to meet them," he added, because he didn't want there to be any more confusion about that.

Tate pondered that for a moment and apparently saw nothing too dangerous. Another thing he really liked about her was that she had a hard time holding a grudge—at least, once she got it out of her system. She entertained him on so many levels. She was quick to laugh and find the humor in things. She was also loyal and funny and easily hurt. Thanks went to Dana for that last fresh bit of insight. The emotional G-force Tate generated was the mental equivalent of riding a bull. There was no mystery involved as to how he felt about that.

"I'm sorry, too. I shouldn't have made that comment about the condoms," she said.

"Hey, now who's the heathen? Although you saved me from a conversation with my mother that I did not want to have, so no apology required."

She nestled under his arm and laid her cheek on his chest. A deep sigh escaped her, as if she'd let go of a long list of worries and could finally relax. "Thank you."

Miles didn't bother asking what for. This was new territory for him. He didn't want to push too hard and too soon for a relationship that went beyond sex. He wrapped both arms around her and rested his chin on her crown while they sat for a while and soaked up the peace, something Tate seemed in need of.

Chapter Twelve

Tate

TATE CLEARED A spot in the living room for the tree while Miles scavenged through the cupboards in search of food. He withdrew a box of macaroni and cheese and threw a tutting noise of disapproval her way.

"It's like teenagers live here," he said.

"You could always have dinner with your parents."

"No, no… we're good. I love macaroni and cheese."

A warm glow spread through Tate. When Miles found out Maybe and Merry planned to decorate a tree, he'd insisted on coming along. *"To make sure you get it right,"* he'd said.

She was so happy to have him here. What a difference a few hours could make. This morning, she'd been a phone call away from telling him he could do to himself what she'd done to Santa. She didn't know where things stood between them, but it was safe to assume more condoms would be required.

But she wondered where his parents' infatuation with

their new granddaughter left her job for the next week or so, since they planned to stay in Grand for the rodeo, and Miles would likely go home to Texas with them for Christmas now that he had nothing to hide.

She didn't want to think too hard about what Christmas in Grand would be like without him to help make spirits bright, but regardless, the Shannahans were about to take their first steps toward forging new Christmas traditions. If she couldn't stop Christmas from coming, then she'd see that it arrived on terms she could live with. Their parents wanted to stay in Florida, play bingo, and learn how to golf? Fine, but it wasn't for Tate.

Maybe and Merry arrived as they were putting their supper dishes away.

Miles took one look at the sisters and turned to Tate. "When Mrs. Quinn said her daughters were identical twins, she wasn't kidding."

"Multiply these two by three," Tate said. "They all look alike. This one is Maybe." She pointed to the twin carrying a box overflowing with garland. "The other is Meredith. Everyone calls her Merry." Merry carried a cookie tin wrapped with a red bow. "They aren't hard to tell apart once you get to know them." The twins might be identical in appearance, but personality-wise, they couldn't be less alike.

Neither one could contain her surprise at the sight of Miles Decker doing dishes in the cramped trailer kitchen, however. He slung the damp cup towel over the oven's door handle and went to shake hands.

"I hope you ladies don't object to me crashing your party," he said, flashing them the famous smile that had won over legions of bull-riding fans across the whole country. If the twins' awed expressions were anything to go by, the damaged left cheek didn't detract from his magnetic appeal for them any more than it had for Tate.

Maybe, the more outgoing sister, spoke for them. As usual.

"You've been holding out on me," she said to Tate. "Traitor. We're supposed to be friends. Wait until I meet Jordan Rowe and see if I give you the details." She'd had an unapologetic crush on the rising country star since she'd first seen him on YouTube, and she sang his songs relentlessly. And hopelessly off-key. And usually with the wrong lyrics.

Ford's arrival interrupted her before she could fully warm up.

Finding Maybe and Meredith in his home was business as usual as far as he was concerned. Miles's presence raised his eyebrows but didn't make him curious enough to ask questions. He untied his boots and left them in the tray by the door, right next to Maybe's more stylish black ankle stilettos.

"Hannah gave me the night off. Private party tonight for the medical clinic," he said to Tate, ignoring the guests, who were clearly Tate's problem, not his. "Dallas is helping her out."

The party was for Dallas's staff, and he liked to wait on them himself. Tate thought it was a nice gesture, and so did his staff, because they loved working for him. Ford got paid regardless, so he liked it, too.

"Come help us decorate the tree," Maybe said to him, because being ignored was so not her thing.

Ford looked at Tate. *She's kidding me, right?*

"Merry made shortbread cookies," Tate said, knowing Ford couldn't resist them. They were his favorite and Merry could cook. "If you want some, you have to earn them."

Miles held up a handful he'd pilfered from the tin and took a bite out of one. "Fresh from the oven and worth it," he mumbled, his mouth full of frosting and cookie. "Melt in your mouth. Just like butter."

Ford was outnumbered and knew it. He peered into the garland-stuffed box on the kitchen table as if he'd been asked to string the rope at his own hanging. "What have you got for decorations?"

"Maybe and Merry brought extras, since all of our Christmas stuff is in storage," Tate said.

"Not all of it. I kept a few things." Ford disappeared down the narrow hall to the bedrooms and returned a few minutes later with a long, flat storage container on wheels, the kind meant for hiding things under a bed. Tate wanted to cry when she saw what he'd saved. He opened the container and began passing out cheap, ugly Christmas sweaters. "If we're doing this, we're doing it right."

Maybe pulled a thin, acrylic sweater on over her shirt, then studied the two reindeer who were engaged in a questionable act on her chest. "Mom should stock these in her shop."

"Hey. You have your Christmas traditions, we have ours," Ford said. "Just because they aren't classy doesn't mean they aren't fun."

"Those reindeer are having fun, alright," Miles said. The black sweater he'd drawn had a snowman on it that looked more like a giant white pumpkin. "Where did you find these?"

"Tanner and I used to pick them up in thrift stores when we were on the road." Tate hadn't known the tradition meant anything to Ford. He'd always worn whatever sweater they gave him, but never said much one way or another. She wanted to hug him for keeping them. Later though, when they were alone.

Maybe was looking at Ford as if they'd never met. "You just used the word fun in a sentence. Are you sure you know what it means?"

Ford's left eyebrow twitched. "I know what it means. I choose to be discreet in its use."

And suddenly, Tate—whose sweater was Pepto Bismol pink and covered in candy canes—wondered if her friend might not be wasting her time on him, after all.

Merry was sorting through ornaments and adding tiny wire hangers to any that had them missing. Her gray sweater featured grumpy cats wearing bright red, stocking hats. As far as ugly went, it wasn't too bad.

"I hear you ladies have plenty of nieces and nephews," Miles said to Merry, drawing her into the conversation, and making Tate like him more than she already did. Even though equally as pretty, and not really shy, Merry often got overshadowed by her more outgoing twin. "I have a five-year-old and three-year-old to buy presents for and no idea what to get them. Any suggestions?"

Merry gave the question a moment of quiet reflection. "How about a toy mechanical bull and practice chute? Raiden sells them."

Miles looked at Tate. "You know her better than I do. Is she serious?"

"She is. Why not get it?" Tate said. "It's a toy, not Bodacious. No worse than a trampoline. Let them get it out of their systems while they're still little. But are you sure their parents won't mind?"

"I'm counting on them having strenuous objections," Miles said. "That's the whole fun of the gift—I get to be the awesome uncle and they get to be jealous of me for my awesomeness."

"As long as you're giving it to them for the right reasons," Tate said.

Maybe passed a handful of white mini lights to Ford to untangle but addressed Miles. "I hear you're riding in the rodeo next weekend."

"I am."

He answered Maybe, but his eyes were on Tate. Her heart hiccupped under her ribs. She concentrated on centering the small tree in front of the window so that its best side was forward. Miles probably thought him riding was an issue for her. It was and it wasn't. She had no serious worries about the rodeo and its safety overall. Participants were there for prize money, not points. Proceeds went to charity and Miles would bring in the numbers.

But she didn't think she could watch. She didn't think she was ready. And she didn't know how to tell him.

The tree looked nice when it was finished. It was the right size for the small room. "Not like that monster you feed live chickens to," she said to Miles. "Any small mammals go missing in your neighborhood yet?"

Miles's eyes warmed with humor. He nudged her with his elbow. "There's nothing wrong with my tree. It leaves Iris alone."

"For now."

"Speaking of Iris…" He checked the time on his phone. "She'll be in bed, which gives my parents too much time on their hands. I should be going."

Tate shrugged into Ford's oversized pea coat and walked Miles to his truck. The inky night sky was peppered in white, and when she gazed up, the whole world spun beneath it. The cold bit at her nose.

She thrust her hands deep into the coat's bulky pockets,

unsure of the best note for ending this evening, given how the day had begun. Keeping things light should be safe. When she spoke, her breath puffed out white. "Good luck with your parents."

"My parents will be fine. My dad's already over it. My mom's going to forgive me eventually. If anyone needs luck, it's going to be you. I'm her baby and nobody's good enough for me."

"I see... I'm the toy mechanical bull you're giving her for Christmas."

"You catch on fast." He put his arms around her and kissed her. "Are you okay with me riding? You got a little quiet after Maybe brought it up."

"Are you kidding? Why wouldn't I be? I'll get to see Miles Decker ride live."

"O-M-G, *Miles Decker* will be there?" He clasped his hands to his chest, doing such a great fan-girl impression that Tate started to laugh. The hiccups in her chest eased, then disappeared.

He kissed her again, drawing it out as if reluctant to let her go, or to have the night end. She felt the same way. He took everything that seemed wrong and spun it on its hind quarters until it was right.

"I'd like you to come to dinner with my parents at my house tomorrow night," he said. "I realize we aren't at the 'meet the parents' stage yet, but that barn door was thrown wide open this morning. They're understandably curious."

Tate had once held a mare for a live cover breeding. She'd sworn never to do it again, but if given a choice between that and dinner with Miles's parents, right now she'd make an exception. "I guess I can't blame them for having concerns about the kind of babysitter you'd hire. Your reputation isn't the best."

"Hey. Mine is no worse than yours. At least I've never made Santa cry."

"They don't know about that." And hopefully, no one would tell them.

"I doubt if the Santa story would make a greater impression on them than seeing you breezing out of the bedroom wearing my shirt without any panties."

And she'd thought the Santa story would be hard to live down. If this one got out, she'd have to leave town. "How about if I show up for dessert and we make mine to go?"

"It's only dinner, Tate. No one is going to demand that you make an honest man out of me. Bring Ford along, if you like. He'll make my mother think twice about discussing condoms with us."

"You'd better hope." Ford preferred not to know what his little sister did when he wasn't around. She massaged her eyes. "This won't end well. You're aware of that. Right?"

"It's just…" He paused, selecting his words. "I'd like my parents to believe I'm capable of maintaining a relationship with a woman for more than a night. I'll make this up to you after they leave."

Tate wasn't sure what to think about that. Was he interested in building something between them, or was the show for his parents? Did she really want to overanalyze this? She'd known what she was doing when she slept with him, and how long it was likely to last. "Remember the Shannahan family Christmas motto—it doesn't have to be classy to be fun."

"That's going on a T-shirt." He gave her one last, lingering kiss, and as he hopped in his truck, Tate heard him singing.

"Sleigh bells ring, are you listening?"

Yes. Yes, she was.

She was too old to believe in the magic of Christmas. But the brief respite from the grind of everyday life that the season provided? Why not ride that polar express for the few weeks it lasted? Reality would return soon enough.

She waited until his truck rounded a bend and passed out of sight. When she turned to head inside, the lights from the tree lit up the front of the trailer and blazed into the night, a glow of hope riding their tails.

Tomorrow's dinner aside, her fresh start with Christmas was showing potential. The only thing missing from this year's winter wonderland was the snow, and honestly, she didn't care about that.

Chapter Thirteen

Miles

M ILES HAD MEANT it when he told Tate that he wanted his parents to know he was capable of a relationship that lasted more than one night. But he also wanted them to see how great she was, too. That was why he experienced a moment of panic when he opened the door.

It quickly shifted to amusement. Tate, in typical Tate style, had taken the new Shannahan motto to heart and was wearing the ugly Christmas sweater with the copulating reindeer on it over a pair of black leggings and thigh-high black boots. She looked like a blond-ponytailed, pornographic Christmas card model.

And young. She looked very young.

Ford had accepted the invitation to dinner, which was a shock in itself. He cleaned up nice. Shock number two. He wore a white sweater and black jeans and looked kind of *GQ* and less terrifying, although he had to duck his head to get through the door, so there was that. He had to be six feet and five or six inches tall, at the least. Likely the only reason he hadn't taken to bull riding, or another extreme sport, was the potential for whiplash. Plus, gear was hard to find for someone his size.

Miles's father emerged from the kitchen where his mother was cooking. He carried Iris, who'd decided her grandpa was only a very small step down from her dad. There was also a very real possibility that Iris simply preferred men. She took one look at Ford—who'd once run three bikers, who were hassling Hannah, out of the taproom by smiling at them—and held out her arms.

Miles's dad didn't know what to do. Neither did Ford.

"Oh, for heaven's sake," Tate said. "Come here, sweetie." She swooped in and plucked Iris from his dad, kissed her cheek and hugged her for a moment, then passed her to Ford, who had no choice but to accept her.

"Dad, this is Tate's brother, Ford Shannahan. Ford, this is my dad. Vince Decker."

"Pleased to meet you," his dad said, extending a hand. Ford awkwardly shook it, trying hard not to break the tiny bundle he held. "I see the family resemblance."

Sure. They both had blond hair and blue eyes. Beyond that, it was up for debate. Miles wanted to bang his head on a wall. Wasn't this going well?

And then his mother arrived on the scene, wiping her hands on a cup towel. Where she'd found the apron, Miles had no idea. She channeled her inner June Cleaver, who emerged during the holidays and for church suppers. The rest of the year she specialized in ordering off menus.

"What a pretty sweater," she said to Tate, and Miles hoped she was being polite and wouldn't figure out what those reindeer were up to during dinner when she had food in her mouth.

"Thank you," Tate said.

Miles introduced his mother to Ford.

"Let me take her off your hands," his mother said, reaching for Iris, and Ford passed her over willingly enough and with obvious relief.

Iris, apparently unused to rejection despite the woman who'd birthed her trying to cure her of that, was not impressed by the transaction. She started to cry.

Meanwhile, Ford tried to distract someone—Miles wasn't sure who—by changing the subject. He admired the tree. "You buy that from Paul Bunyan?" he asked.

"Ha, ha," Miles said. "This from the guy who could pass for Paul Bunyan's clone. I need a drink. Let me get you a beer."

"I'll give you a hand in the kitchen," Tate said to his mother, and Miles experienced a fresh wave of fear.

"Let's all have drinks in the kitchen," he said.

His mother patted his arm. "Don't be silly. You men have your drinks in front of the tree. Put on some music. Let Tate and I get to know each other. Dinner will be ready in a few minutes."

His mom had taught him to cook, but she could fake old

school when it suited her purpose, and right now it did. Meanwhile, Tate was being unnervingly agreeable, because it was unlike her to hang out in the kitchen while the men lazed around drinking beer.

When his mom called the men into the kitchen a half an hour later, Tate was busy setting wineglasses on the table—which looked very festive, with a white linen tablecloth, red candles, and bud vases stuffed with pinecones and dried grasses. As far as he could tell, everything seemed fine between them.

"So, Tate," his mom began when they'd all filled their plates with steak, roasted vegetables, and bread. "Tell us a little about yourself. How did you end up babysitting for Miles? Is this a career choice or are you earning money for college?"

"Mom!" Miles said sharply. "If you want to know how old she is, ask me later."

Tate smiled at him, then his mother, and left the age issue alone. "It's neither. A friend told me he was looking for someone to take care of his daughter, and I'm a big fan, so I applied for the job."

Miles sensed danger and rushed in to help save her from drowning. "Tate's not that kind of fan."

"What kind of fan would that be, dear?" his mother asked, sounding innocent enough, but he'd gotten plenty of lectures on that particular topic and he wasn't fooled.

"He means I'm not a buckle bunny," Tate cheerfully inserted, and Ford coughed up the sip of wine he'd just taken. The table jerked and Tate jumped, leading Miles to the conclusion that her brother had kicked her beneath it.

His mom had presided over plenty of family dinners, and it took more than a kick under the table to faze her. She resumed questioning Tate as if nothing had happened. "You're good with Iris. You must have had quite a bit of childcare experience."

"Mm," Tate said, shoveling food in her mouth.

Smooth. Miles took a long swig out of his own glass of wine. He hadn't considered how the evening would likely progress when he'd agreed to invite her to dinner.

"Tate's good at looking after people," Ford said unexpectedly. He cut his meat into small, precise pieces, all the same size, and kept his eyes on his plate while he spoke. "Particularly when she cares about them. She's a typical Demeter archetype. A nurturer and overcontrolling mother figure." Everyone stared at him. And then, because a penchant for unfiltered honesty must run in the family, he added, "She's a terrible cook, though. She never caught on to that."

Miles filed the archetype information away. Nurturing fit with what he'd heard about her and what he'd seen for himself. It also explained why she'd taken the hit from her parents over her brother's death. They hadn't fully grasped the dangers of bull riding and assumed she'd look out for him as usual.

Nah. Miles dismissed that line of thinking as giving them far too much credit. Her parents were self-absorbed jerks, and nothing would convince him otherwise.

He wasn't about to let Ford outdo him when it came to defending his sister, however. His reputation was on the line here as well. Did his mother think he'd let just anyone look after his daughter, simply because they claimed to be one of his fans?

"Tate came highly recommended," he said.

As far as defending her honor went, it wasn't heroic. But it did serve the purpose, which was to make his mother back down.

She dabbed at her lips with her napkin, then angled a hand toward Tate and patted the table between them. "I'm not surprised. You're doing a wonderful job, dear. Iris is happy and seems well looked after. I have no complaints."

"Why not lead with that, then?" Miles said, exasperated now, and discovered kicking people under the table was a Shannahan thing when the toe of Tate's boot connected with his ankle.

Dinner finally ended. Thank Jesus. Ford went outside to warm up the truck. Miles left his parents in the kitchen and cornered Tate at the front door. He slid the pocket door to the living room closed.

"I'm sorry about that," he said.

Tate drifted into his arms and touched his cheek. "Why? They love you. It's sweet."

He loved it when she touched him like this. And when she looked into his eyes the way she was now.

"My parents want to look after Iris this week," he said. "That means you get a week off with pay. But they asked if you'd help with her the day of the rodeo. Pretty sure they just want to get to know you when I'm not around, so don't say you weren't warned. You can sit with them in the stands."

He'd be lying if he said he wasn't looking forward to her fangirling over his ride. He couldn't wait.

Outside, Ford leaned on the horn, letting Tate and the whole neighborhood know he was ready to leave.

Miles opened the door and held it for her. He kissed her as she brushed past him. "I'll call you."

She kissed him back. It was demanding and sweet, all wrapped into one. "And you'll sing to me, right?"

Miles laughed and shoved her out the door. He waited until she was safely in the truck, then closed it. He turned. His mom and dad were standing behind him.

"I like her," his mom said.

"Me, too," Miles replied.

"But that sweater she's wearing is awful," she added. "Does she know what those reindeer are doing?"

Chapter Fourteen

Tate

TATE HADN'T FORGOTTEN the electric excitement of an arena as the announcers worked the crowd, and these announcers were good.

The Endeavour had done everything about this rodeo right, in large part thanks to Miles. The light display alone was spectacular. Blinding strobes sprayed the bleachers and bounced off hundreds of eager faces. Combined with the chest-pounding music that thrummed through the arena, the day was off to a great start.

She'd made it into the bleachers without passing out, mostly because this venue was far different from the last one she'd attended. For starters, this was an unsanctioned event. The riders were here for the show and to gain experience, not to earn points. Injuries were par for the course but would likely involve little more than a few cuts and bruises, because the bullfighters were professionals even if the riders were not. She had no real worries for Miles. There wasn't a bull in these pens that he couldn't stick.

And yet she couldn't relax. Anxiety crawled through her chest and rumbled around inside her head. She hadn't heard a word Helen said since they sat down.

"Isn't this exciting? It's been nearly three years since I last saw Miles ride," his mother shouted over the pulsating beat of the music.

Tate smiled at her pride in her son, because what else could she do? A few years ago, she would have been thrilled to see Miles ride live, too, even if this wasn't a pro event. She rubbed her hands on her thighs and tried not to squirm. She'd stick it out.

The first bull entered the chute. The boy about to ride him had to be eighteen at the most. Tate closed her eyes and didn't open them until the shrill blare of the whistle signaled the end of his ride and the crowd began cheering.

Helen was watching her with puzzled concern. "Are you okay, dear?"

"A little tired," Tate said. She didn't dare close her eyes again, so when the next rider and bull came out of the chute, she fixed on a point in the stands and let her eyesight go blurry.

The second and third riders came and went. One lasted three seconds. The other took a hoof to the shoulder, which tore his shirt, but the bull had no further interest in him, and he'd have nothing to show for it but a scrape and a bruise.

The fourth rider lasted the full eight seconds. The whistle blew and the crowd expressed their appreciation His bull, however, had a bad attitude. It didn't like the rider and it wasn't fond of one of the bullfighters either, taking turns going after both men. The remaining three bullfighters formed a triangle to draw the bull's attention away from its targets while the first bullfighter hustled the rider into the safety chute.

A hush fell over the crowd. Dana's screams replayed in Tate's head. Pressure built with the intensity of a corked, boiling kettle against the top of her skull. Seconds dragged into an eternity before the signal came that the men were fine. Loud victory music boomed from the speakers.

Tate couldn't stand another minute of it. Her head continued to pound.

"The noise level can't be good for a baby's ears," she said to Miles's mother. "I'll take Iris back to the bunkhouse."

Helen looked surprised but didn't argue about it as Tate gathered Iris's diaper bag and stroller and left.

Miles

MILES LOVED EVERYTHING about competition. He loved the vibe from the crowds. The music. The food in the concourse. He'd grown up on that stuff.

And he was pleased with the way the day had progressed. He could—and would—build this rodeo into something the town could be proud of, not just the Endeavour. He'd put Grand on the pro rodeo map.

He pulled on his glove and adjusted his helmet, making extra sure of the fit. He gathered his rope and reined in his eagerness. He was riding for show, and he'd give the crowd one, but he had to get his head in the right place and keep it there until the ride was over.

He climbed the rail and hovered over the bull in the chute, careful not to let his legs get pinned if it fought. He'd drawn Prince Charming, the oldest and toughest competitor, which made him happy, but he suspected Ryan had rigged it. Prince Charming knew what he liked and what he didn't. He did not like the flank strap and he liked riders no better.

But he was a season or two past his prime and he wasn't known as a twister. Miles was going to see what he could do about that. He settled onto the bull's back, sensing his mood through the flinching and twitching of muscles. He gave a nod to Levi Harrington, who was manning the chute, and Levi opened the gate.

Prince Charming exploded, but from the second Miles got on his back, he was in charge. His free arm went up. He had the bull rope in his gloved hand under control. His seat was well-balanced, and he moved as if he were an extension of the bull. He had eight seconds to whip up the crowd and give them what they'd paid for, so he gave Prince Charming a light nudge with his spurs.

Prince Charming's response surpassed expectations. His

hind end gyrated to the left in an attempt to join up with his front. Miles had made an accurate guess as to the direction he'd spin, so when a horn nicked his knee, he was ready for it. The bruise it left behind would be nothing.

The whistle blew. Miles hit the ground running, dodging flying hooves as he made a dash for the rails so the bullfighters would have room to work. Then, it was over. The bull trotted back to the pens and the gate closed behind it.

Miles threw his arms in the air and soaked up the appreciative roar of the fans. This was the most fun he'd had in months, and he'd loved every one of those too-brief eight seconds. The best part of the whole ride was having Tate here to see it. The way her eyes lit up when she looked at him was worth more than cheers for a has-been from strangers.

He scanned the bleachers where she sat with his parents, hoping to witness her excitement for him firsthand, but her seat was empty. A little of his pleasure trickled away, replaced by a thin layer of disappointment. Where was she? Had she missed his ride?

He'd have to sort it out later. Until then he had interviews to field, a few photos to pose for, and autographs to sign. There would be a quick debrief with his boss as to how the bull riding event went since it was the highlight of the day and what the ranch was focused on.

It was an hour before he made it into the bleachers and found his parents patiently waiting for him. They were used to the routine and knew to let him come to them, but they weren't who he looked for this time.

"Where's Tate?" he asked, then panic hummed in his head because Iris wasn't here, either. What if something had happened to her? "Where's Iris?"

"Iris is fine," his mother said. "I would have dragged you off that bull myself to let you know if she wasn't. Tate took her to the bunkhouse to get her away from the noise. She thought it was too much for a baby."

That made sense, except he'd begun to think Iris was hard of hearing because of her ability to sleep through the confusion of everyday life at the ranch house.

"Tate seemed a little off, though," his mom added. "She's not coming down with something, is she?"

His dad shot him a sharp, questioning, *what-the-hell* look over his mother's head.

"She's not pregnant, Dad." He'd be years living that down. "I'll go check on them. Enjoy the rest of the show." He'd learned his love for the sport from his parents and they'd come all this way. There was no need for them to miss any of it.

The barrelman, dressed up as Santa, with ponies in antlers hitched up to his sleigh, raced his makeshift reindeer around the arena while tossing out candy to the crowd. The high school cheerleading squad was also scheduled to perform, and after that, a local country singer who'd been making a name in Nashville for himself.

Getting out of the arena was no easy task.

"Miles!" a woman called out.

He turned automatically to have a camera thrust in his face. Great. Another reporter, right when he was in a hurry. But the public was his bread and butter, so he pulled out his famous smile, slapped it in place, and prepared for the usual questions.

"Was it difficult, getting back on a bull?"

"Most natural thing in the world," he replied.

"Think you'll ever return to the circuit?"

"Not a chance. I'm too old for that level of competition. I'll leave it to the young guys."

"Tell us a bit about what life has been like after your accident. I understand you have a new daughter."

Miles felt his smile tighten but he kept it in place. "I do."

"What about her mother? Was that her, sitting with your parents in the bleachers?"

He should have seen that question coming. "No comment."

"Her name is Tate Shannahan, isn't it?" the reporter persisted. "Wasn't her brother killed in a bull riding accident last year? She didn't stay for your ride. How does she feel about you returning to the sport, especially after your own accident?"

She had to work for the tabloids, because this wasn't news—this was how rumors got started. He couldn't think of a way to get out of the interview without making it worse than it was.

"No comment," he said again, and this time, he kept walking.

He wished he'd handled those questions better. The story pieced together from them was not going to be pretty. And now he had to put more thought into how Tate felt about him riding, and if maybe he'd done something insensitive, when what he'd set out to do was impress her.

When he got to the bunkhouse, Tate was on the floor playing with Iris. Toys were scattered around them. They looked up and smiled, each equally sweet, and his heart twisted like Prince Charming's ride.

Why hadn't Tate stuck around?

"What happened to you?" he asked.

She got to her feet. "Nothing. Iris was tired. It was loud and she couldn't sleep, so I decided to leave and let your parents enjoy the show."

She'd lied to him. Iris could sleep through a tornado if she was tired. The lie annoyed him. "Don't tell me you're okay with something when clearly, you're not. If you didn't want me to ride you should have said so."

Her gaze cooled, letting him know that if he wanted to pick a fight, she'd give him one. "I was fine with you riding. I wasn't worried about you. It's not always about you, you know."

The tight knot of worry inside him unwound. This was better. They were going to get this out in the open, once and for all. Tate had serious hang-ups about her brother's death, and while those weren't going to go away overnight, she didn't get to blame herself anymore, so he pushed her a little. "If you weren't worried about me, then what's the problem?"

"It sounds so stupid."

"Try me."

"I was worried about *me*." She slapped her hand on the table. "I have panic attacks every time I get close to an arena. I can't stop them. I can't predict them. They're embarrassing and they make me mad at myself. There. Are you happy?" She was shouting at him. She slammed the table again.

Iris burst into tears. He moved to pick her up, but Tate brushed him aside. She gathered Iris in her arms and cuddled her close. Which one of them she was trying to comfort, Miles couldn't say. When had he gotten so bad at handling women? Or was it just Tate?

"I'm sorry, sweetie," she crooned to Iris. "I'm not mad at you. I'm mad at your father for making me mad. And that makes me mad at myself because I shouldn't have let him make me so mad."

"That's a lot of being mad at yourself," Miles said. "You can be madder at me, if you like. You know… maybe spread it around more. Thin it out."

Tate glared at him in a way that made him wonder if Santa had seen it coming the way he saw it now. And then all the fight drained out of her. A reluctant smile curved her lips—like the sun breaking dawn after a stormy night. "I told you it was stupid."

He took Iris from her and settled her in the playpen. The baby sniffled a little, undecided as to whether she should settle down or rekindle the drama. "I'll buy you a pony if you stop crying," he said to her.

"You might want to save that bribe for when she's older," Tate said.

"When she's older she'll remember I said it. Then I'll have to produce a pony."

Tate's expression said *you can't be serious.* "You're going to give her one anyway."

"Yeah. I am." He couldn't wait to teach Iris to ride. A pony, though. Not a bull. He reached for Tate, who looked more in need of immediate consoling. "Come here. Let's talk about how stupid you are."

"I never said I was stupid. I said my *reason* was stupid."

He kissed her forehead. "It's okay to have panic attacks. They won't last forever, you know. But if they're out of control you should see someone. Athletes see sport psychologists all the time. It's nothing to feel stupid about."

"When did you last see a sport psychologist?"

"What... me? Never. Do I seem stupid to you?" Her body laugh over that shook him, too, and he held her tight so he could enjoy it. "Kidding. I went to see one right before I quit the sport. I talked through my reasons for getting out. It helped me confirm that I'd made the right decision so I could look back on my career with no regrets."

Her laughter subsided. "I don't want to see a sport psychologist."

"Then don't. You can talk it through with me, if you like. It's your choice. I didn't go see a psychologist after my accident either. The bull was being a bull and I was careless. Simple as that."

Tate, back on track now that she'd blown off some steam, discovered something new to be bothered about. Of course.

Disappointment brewed in her eyes. "I missed your ride."

"I noticed." Because he'd wanted her there, damn it. He really liked it when she admired him.

"I had a chance to see *Miles Decker* ride live and I *missed* it."

"It was spectacular, too. I was amazing," he said, rubbing it in.

"I doubt it. Prince Charming has a seventy-two buck-off percent. If you couldn't stick that ride, I'd be embarrassed for you."

He edged a few steps closer toward falling in love. She might admire him, but she was realistic about it. She was lovely and complex, and he never knew which way she'd twist. At the end of the day, if there was one ride he intended to stick, winning Tate over was it.

"Oh, and by the way," he said. "Here's a quick heads-up. There might be a story circulating that you're my baby mama."

"I want a raise," Tate said.

Chapter Fifteen

Tate

MORNING FROST, NOT yet chased off by the sun, slicked the railing and steps when Tate answered a knock on the trailer door.

Helen's bright, personable, *let's-be-friends* smile rivaled her son's. "I hope you don't mind my stopping by so early."

"Of course not. Come in," Tate said, even though she'd been cleaning the bathroom and wasn't at a personal best.

"Your tree is lovely." Helen politely focused on the highlights of the home rather than any shortcomings she observed. While the trailer was neat and tidy enough, calling it shabby was kind.

"Thank you."

Tate wondered what had brought on this visit. Helen seemed nice enough on the surface but remained somewhat distant with her. Understandable, really. Iris was likely the only girl in Miles's life his family felt safe becoming attached to.

Helen talked about the rodeo's success while Tate put on

coffee. "It's a shame you missed Miles's ride," she concluded, enforcing Tate's suspicion she was fishing for something.

"I'm sorry I missed it, too," Tate said. "Like I said, I've been a huge fan of his for years."

"He seems to be a big fan of yours as well."

Tate wasn't adept at sorting out subtext, but even she had a good idea of where this conversation was headed. "We haven't known each other long enough for him to be serious about me, if that's what you mean."

"I see… How serious are you about him?"

Reading that subtext didn't take a whole lot of skill. *Serious enough to sleep with him, wouldn't you say?* Miles might have gotten his looks from his dad but the steely focus that kept him on the back of a bull came from his five-feet-tall mom. Tate began to sympathize with how he'd felt about the condom discussion.

"I feel the same way he does, in that. It's too soon to tell."

"Good," his mother said. "Because he's got this stubborn idea he wants to stay in Grand for Christmas, and I worried you might be the reason behind it. His father and I think he should bring Iris home so the family can meet her. I'd like the chance to spoil my new granddaughter a little."

Tate didn't hear much about what Miles might want in what his mother was saying, but she understood Helen's desire to have her family together for Christmas. If Tate could have one thing under the tree, she'd ask for that, too.

"Iris is easy to love," she said, doing her best to steer clear of any landmines.

"She certainly is. Miles was like that as a baby. So cuddly and sweet." Helen took a sip of her coffee, then got to the point. "I hoped you might be willing to speak to him about flying home to Texas with us for the holidays."

Sharp disappointment took a bite out of Tate's heart.

"What he chooses to do is none of my business," she said. "But he seemed insistent that he wanted to start new traditions here. He was excited about putting up his own tree." Decorating it with him had been so much fun, too, but she set that bit of wistfulness aside. This wasn't about her. It was about what Miles really wanted and what was best for him and Iris.

"Only because he didn't know how to tell us about Iris. Which is no longer a problem. And why I thought you might be the real reason."

He'd made up his mind to stay here before they'd gotten involved. But he'd spoken so warmly of Christmas in Texas. Why shouldn't he and Iris go home and enjoy it with family? Her relationship with her own parents was strained enough that she didn't want to come between him and his. "It's not because of me."

"Then you won't mind me telling him how unreasonable he's being and that you're fine with him coming to Texas with us?" Helen pressed.

"Not at all," Tate said, because of course she was fine

with it. Why wouldn't she be?

TATE TOOK A drive to the ranch after lunch. The frozen surface of the Tongue River sparkled through the naked cottonwood trees. She counted five bald eagles hunched in their branches.

A bag with Iris's Christmas gift in it sat on the passenger seat. The gift wasn't expensive, but she'd put a lot of thought into it, and it was as much for Miles as his daughter, although only she would know that. They hadn't discussed exchanging gifts and she didn't want it to be weird.

She parked near the barns and was halfway to the arena where Miles had said he'd be working when Ryan O'Connell emerged from one of the outbuildings and fell into step.

"Got a minute?" he said.

This must be Tate's day for attracting undesirable conversations.

She had reservations about Ryan. She wasn't afraid of him. She'd grown up around Ford and Ford was a tough act to beat. It was more that she held him in awe. Her tongue tripped over itself when he was around, and her hands and feet never seemed to know where they should be. He reminded her of a cowboy Bruce Wayne—slick and smooth on the outside, but with an alter ego vigilante inside. Laws didn't apply to men like him. He didn't generate panic attacks, but neither did he settle her nerves. Not the way Miles did.

"Sure," she said, because she couldn't say no to him any more than she'd been able to brush off Miles's mother—which illustrated how unfair her reputation for being difficult to get along with really was.

"Miles speaks highly of you," Ryan began, in a tone of voice that usually led to some sort of *but*. She had a gut-churning flashback to the day she'd been fired. *Thank you, Santa.* Did she work for Miles or the Endeavour? Did the ranch have a policy about employee fraternization? How had Ryan found out?

"I can explain."

"Really?" He looked taken aback. "Please do."

For the love of Pete, Tate. Do you even listen to what people say before you speak up? Miles speaks highly of you. *How are you supposed to explain* that?

"He's happy to have found someone to look after Iris so close to Christmas, when everyone is busy. And I live nearby, which is a bonus." That was the best she could come up with. And yes, she was aware of how lame it sounded.

If Ryan agreed, she couldn't tell. He stuck to business. "How do you like babysitting?"

"I love it," Tate said, speaking with more confidence because she could be honest. "Iris is a sweetheart. Miles is easy to please." She replayed her words in her head. Her face grew hot enough to melt the Tongue River from Grand all the way to Wyoming. "I mean, Miles is easy to work for."

"Do you like working at the ranch, too?"

"I do," she said warily. Where was this conversation headed? Was she about to be fired?

Now that the rodeo was over, maybe he expected her to look after Iris at Miles's house in Grand and not at the ranch.

"Elizabeth suggested you might be interested in a more permanent position," Ryan said. "We'd talked about opening a daycare for employees on the ranch, and with a baby of our own on the way, the timing is right. We'll have to explore childcare licensing, but Posey McGregor runs a licensed facility in town and she's an excellent resource. We'd pay for any training you require, of course."

A permanent position on the Endeavour Ranch as a daycare provider… Giddiness left Tate light-headed. That sounded a lot more appealing than a seasonal gig as an elf. It sounded like a career. Ford would be pleased—she could pay rent.

But what if things didn't work out between her and Miles? Could she stand it if he began seeing other women? Could they at least remain friends?

She didn't know. She did know she'd miss his companionship. She had tons of casual friends, but her inner circle was tight and exclusive, and he'd worked his way in.

"Can I take a few days to think about it?" she said.

"Take all the time you need."

Ryan veered off, heading back to the barns, leaving her to finish the walk to the arena alone. She waited for the familiar panicky sensation to set in, but it didn't happen. She trusted Miles to know what he was doing, she realized, only somewhat surprised. He understood the mentalities of the riders and bulls, and their safety was his priority, not cutting costs. The rodeo workers he hired were the best.

It also helped to hear him insist that her brother had ridden by choice, not because she'd held any sway in his decisions other than to serve as his manager and get him signed up for events that furthered his career. Tanner hadn't been very businesslike in that regard. All he'd wanted to do was ride.

Acknowledging it took the edge off the pain and the guilt. Someday, she'd forgive herself. She wasn't quite there yet. And she doubted if she'd ever be able to sit and watch another bull riding event that Miles hadn't engineered.

The arena was empty. She found Miles in his small office near the locker and medical rooms. He was hunched over a computer keyboard, busy typing what looked like an email.

"Hi," he said, looking both pleased and surprised when she knocked on his door to announce her arrival. "Please tell me you're here so we can sneak in a little alone time together."

He was impossible to resist when he smiled at her that way. She felt good about the gift she had for him. He'd appreciate the thought behind it, and that was what was important.

"Alone time sounds good." She set the gift bag and her purse on a chair. "Ryan asked if I'd like to work at an employee daycare here, at the ranch. Are you okay with it if I accept?"

He circled the desk. "Why wouldn't I be? Because Iris would no longer have your undivided attention? She'd have other kids to play with. I think it's a great idea."

"But what if you and I…" She tried to come up with a delicate way to put it. One that didn't make it sound as if she thought they were doomed.

"What if we can't be friends anymore?" he said, finishing her thought for her.

"Exactly."

"I don't see any reason why we can't remain friends. Do you?"

"No."

But she didn't sound as confident as she would have liked. She wasn't worried about whether they could remain friends based on where they were now. She was more worried about how she'd handle it if Miles became friends with some other lucky woman. She had a history of poor gut reactions to back up her concern.

She picked up the gift bag. "I have a small gift for Iris, and I wanted to give it to you without an audience around."

"What a coincidence." He reached behind him into a drawer on the other side of the desk and withdrew a white envelope with a shiny red bow on it. "Iris has a small gift for you, too." He handed it to her.

The envelope was suspiciously thick. "Should I open it now?" she asked.

"Go ahead."

She ran her finger under the flap, prying the glue loose. The envelope contained a card with money tucked inside it, as she'd suspected. A Christmas bonus was what one would expect from an employer.

Tate didn't pay any attention to the money, although the amount was staggering, considering she'd only worked for him for a few weeks. The card's message was the real gift. *THE BEST PRESENT ONE CAN HOPE FOR THIS YEAR IS TO SPEND TIME TOGETHER.* Next to those words he'd written, *THE MONEY'S FROM IRIS. THE SENTIMENT'S MINE.*

Her eyelashes dampened and she blinked the tears back. She wasn't sure if he knew how much those words meant to her, but he'd chosen the ones she most longed to hear.

"Thank you," she said, embarrassed by her reaction, and he ducked in for a kiss.

"My turn," he said.

He untied the ribbon and set it aside, then peeled the tape off the pretty wrapping paper with care, as if understanding that the effort she'd put into the presentation was as much a part of the gift as the gift itself.

He studied it for so long that she began to have second and third thoughts. Maybe ten. She'd assumed he would get the message. What if he didn't?

"It's a picture of you and Iris," she said, helping him out.

"I can see that."

It was the one she'd taken with her phone the day she'd first toured the arena. Father and daughter gazed at each other as if neither had ever seen anything quite so amazing before. Iris had her small hand on Miles's face. Tate loved the image, but she wasn't the photographer in the family. That talent went to Ford. He'd fiddled around with the image using computer software until it was a real work of art, then she'd had it framed.

"I thought Iris might like to have a memory to keep of how happy you both were when you found each other." And she wanted Miles to see that the way his daughter looked at him had nothing to do with his fame or his scarred face, and everything to do with how wonderful he was, all on his own.

"I have got to start keeping condoms in my desk," he finally said.

"Luckily for you, I've learned a few things from Maybe about planning ahead." She dug the box out of her purse and tossed it to him.

His happy grin turned the bumpy-ridged scar on his cheek into a vee, directing attention to the joyful anticipation in his eyes, and Tate's thigh muscles clenched at the sight. "Hallelujah. Christmas came early."

"About that." She decided to get the main reason she was here out of the way so they could concentrate on exchanging more gifts. She could learn to like this new tradition.

"There you go again, not knowing when to stop talking," he complained. "Either 'I've learned a few things,' or 'planning ahead' would have been good." The dramatic sigh accompanying his words let her know he was kidding. "What's the problem?"

The problem was that she'd have to regift his gift to her, and pass it on to his family, because he really should spend Christmas with them.

"Your mom wants you to take Iris to Texas for Christmas."

"Yes, I'm aware." He played with the box in his hands, then set it beside the photo he'd propped on his desk. "My mom has got to learn to mind her own business."

"You should go."

He was silent for a long moment. "I guess I should have explained Iris's gift to you. Unless you don't want it." His voice held a question.

"I got it. No explanation required," Tate said. "And I want it." Did she ever. "And I know you'd like to start your own traditions here, in your new house, with your new daughter. But Christmas is about being with family and you should give yours this opportunity to get to know their newest member." She cleared crushed rock from her throat. Her family situation had changed forever in less than six seconds, so she knew what she was talking about. "Ford and I have plans to spend Christmas together," she added, proving tact was so not her thing. She made it sound as if their plans didn't include him, when in fact, he and Iris had featured heavily in them.

Right up until this morning.

He leaned on the desk. His smile stayed in place even as the joy died in his eyes. "I suppose there's always next year."

He could be excused for his confusion. She was sending mixed signals again. Plus, she'd ruined his gift to her by insinuating that time spent with Ford was more important to her than time spent with him.

She was so bad at this.

She wriggled her hips between his thighs and rested her hands on his shoulders. She kissed him, putting everything into it that she couldn't find the right words to express.

"Or," she said, touching his cheek, "there's always right now." She let her eyes drift to the condoms and lifted a brow.

"Mm." Miles returned her kiss with enough enthusiasm to unravel the kink in her stomach. His hand slid under her sweater, fingers teasing the sensitive belly piercing, and muscles twitched as she sucked in a breath. He licked her lower lip with the tip of his tongue, and with that added distraction, she forgot what they'd been talking about. "I could get used to this new tradition."

"Me, too," Tate said.

Could she ever.

Chapter Sixteen

Miles

THE GRASS AROUND the terminal was green when Miles walked out of Laredo International Airport with his mom and dad at his side. Heat slapped him in the face. The blue sky and lack of snow were the only things his hometown had in common with Grand.

Airport travel hadn't been as rough as expected. Iris's presence had sparked some interest, especially with airport security, exactly as he'd predicted, because a baby traveling without her mother raised a few flags. Then there had been a few diehard fans at the airport in Billings eager for selfies with him, which he'd provided.

But once they'd touched down in Laredo, it was business as usual. People in his hometown had seen him in person plenty of times.

His mom pushed Iris in her stroller while he and his dad dragged their luggage to the car. Miles couldn't believe how much stuff babies required, and topped off with the gifts he'd bought, a rental might be in order.

He couldn't wait to see his sister's reaction Christmas morning when Sydney and Pax unwrapped the toy mechanical bull he'd bought from Raiden. Anna was going to have a cow.

Something was missing, however.

Not something. Someone. He would have loved to invite Tate along, too, since this was her idea, not his, but she'd wanted to spend Christmas with Ford. He couldn't say how Ford might want to spend Christmas, but it was safe to assume that whatever his preference, Tate played a big part. Ford had made it clear the night they'd had dinner together that he'd hand Miles his ass if he ever hurt her.

They managed to fit everything in his parents' SUV. After that, it was a twenty-minute drive to their house. They had an hour to get settled before heading to his sister's house for the traditional December twenty-third dinner. His mom always hosted Christmas Eve.

Anna and Neil lived in a Spanish-Colonial home with terra-cotta clay tiles on the flat roof and thick, white stucco walls. Carved wooden floors, high wooden beams, and small windows with sturdy wooden shutters completed the theme of a late nineteenth-century house built under a Mexican influence. Spanish was the family's second language, and as familiar as English to him to the point where he often couldn't say what people were speaking without stopping to think.

His arrival was usually greeted with excitement. Not to-

THE COWBOY'S CHRISTMAS BABY

day.

Anna flew past him to snatch Iris from her car seat before anyone else had a chance, as if she'd been lying in wait. Sydney was right behind her, proving women really did have some sort of built-in baby radar from birth.

Neil, Anna's husband, hung back, knowing not to get in his wife's way when there was a baby involved. Pax stood beside him, clinging to his leg, greeting the entire scene and everyone in it with a three-year-old's heightened suspicion. His expression said he didn't care for whatever was going down, and neither did he approve of having his mother's attention hijacked by someone smaller and possibly cuter than him. His eyes shifted to Miles's face and his grip on his dad's leg tightened.

Miles, however, now knew what to expect. Rather than swoop in on Pax the way he normally would, he ignored him and spoke to Neil. "Merry Christmas."

"Thanks. It's going to be an interesting one." Neil gestured toward the car where his wife, daughter, and mother-in-law were wrestling each other for possession of Iris, who might require some sort of crisis intervention before the evening was over. "You really outdid yourself with the gift-giving this year."

"Wait until you see what's under the tree for the kids Christmas morning."

"If it's a horse, you're a dead man."

Miles laughed.

His dad joined them on the steps while the men waited to find out who was the winner in the baby tug-of-war sweepstakes. Pax, by now, had grown tired of being ignored. He patted Miles's knee. Miles crouched on his heels so that he was at his young nephew's eye level.

"I have a pet gecko. His name is Larry," Pax said. He studied Miles's scarred cheek, then reached out to touch it. "He feels like you do."

"Is that a fact?" Miles said. *Yep, still ninety-five percent pretty.* And the last five percent was a one-hundred-percent crowd pleaser for the right audience. "Why don't you show him to me so I can see for myself?"

Pax, happy to be the center of an adult's attention, took his hand and dragged him off to the family room, where Larry had the run of a terrarium that the American Museum of Natural History would envy.

Once Sydney's fascination with Iris faded enough for Anna not to fear for the baby's safety, and they'd finished a dinner of tapas, lentil soup, roast pork, and potatoes, they shared a dessert of fruit and sugared nuts in the living room, where Sydney and Pax got to open their pre-Christmas presents from Miles. He'd picked up candy from the local sweet shop in Grand, as well as two handmade toys. Pax got a wooden agricultural truck with enough intricate moving parts to create a serious choking hazard. Sydney's anatomically correct baby boy doll sported real human hair, a lifelike silicone head and body, and was dressed in an outfit from

Cloda Quinn's store.

"That doll's creepy," Neil said, sipping one of the craft beer Miles had brought him from Hannah's taproom. "If you left it in a hot car, someone would either smash your window in or call the cops on you."

"You're welcome," Miles said.

He helped Anna and Neil carry empty plates to the kitchen while the grandparents kept the children entertained.

Anna was three years older than him and had been on the brink of exploding with questions for hours. She loved to give unsolicited advice—a trait she'd inherited from their father. Her ability to get straight to the point came from their mom.

"What do you know about Iris's mother?" she asked, stacking plates next to the dishwasher.

Not enough for this conversation.

"She's Texan." He was pretty sure about that. "And she's not coming back." Ryan's sources seemed confident enough to make him sure on that, too. The bloodwork might take another few weeks because of the holidays, but he didn't need it. "I met her in a bar. We spent one unmemorable night together."

"Fantastic." Anna let her tone and the roll of her eyes speak her opinion for her. "Why are the news outlets reporting that some bull rider's sister—Tate something-or-other— is Iris's mother?"

Miles didn't make the mistake of calling Tate the

babysitter again. He didn't need another schooling on that from his dad. Besides, it wasn't true. He missed her. He wished she was here. It didn't feel like Christmas without her.

Coming to Texas had been a mistake.

"Wishful thinking," he replied, in response to the question. On everyone's part, including his. "Tate's been more of a mother to Iris than Tami"—one m and an i—"ever wanted to be." Iris was nothing more than a meal ticket to her. He couldn't forget how she'd walked out of his house, leaving an eight-month-old baby with a man she didn't know a whole lot about, without a backward glance or show of regret.

Anna would not let it go. "Tate's been a mother to Iris. What is she to you?"

Miles looked to Neil for assistance. *Hey, man. She's your wife. Help a guy out.*

Neil shrugged, shut the dishwasher door, and backed slowly out of the kitchen as if they'd been confronted by an irate mother bear that showed signs of attacking. *She's your sister, pal. Leave me out of this. You're on your own.*

"I'm going to go out on a limb and guess Mom's been talking to you," Miles said to his sister.

"She has. And after that, I talked to Dad." Anna settled a hip against the counter and made herself comfortable, meaning this discussion might take a while. "Mom was excited about Iris—who is adorable, so good going there— and that you were both coming for Christmas. Brace yourself, by the way. She's looking at houses for you so you can move home. I'm supposed to help her convince you that it's best for Iris if you both stay."

He should have expected as much. "What did Dad have to say?"

"He likes Tate. He says she's perfect for you, and for Iris, but Montana might be a better place for you than Laredo, because otherwise, you'll have two women running your life."

More like he'd have three, counting Anna. Four, if he factored in Iris. Not that he was stupid enough to say it out loud.

But the thought of having Tate running his life didn't sound so very bad. Boundaries were key. The age difference between them might give him a slight edge while they sorted them out.

"What's your opinion?" Because they both knew she had one.

"That things change once kids are involved and your years of screwing around and doing whatever you please are officially over. You need to choose between your job in Grand and moving home to have Mom and me help you take care of Iris. You'll find a job here without any problem, and you'll have help with childcare, so overall that's not a bad option. But you need to make up your mind about Tate, too. Is she the one? And if so, will she want to move to Laredo?"

Those were a lot of decisions. Before Iris, he would have said no to moving home. After she'd been dropped on his doorstep, the possibility had crossed his mind. Once he'd met Tate, however…

The answer became a resounding *hell, no*.

"I've only known her a few weeks," he hedged. This might be a conversation he should have with her first.

"That's a week and five days longer than usual."

"Ouch."

"Look, moron. I knew Neil was the one five minutes after I met him at a friend's party. I nailed him across the back of the head while taking a swing at a pinata and he apologized to me for getting in my way. He smiled and that was it."

"It's no surprise to me that you had to beat him into submission." When had he first suspected Tate might be the one? The answer to that was a no-brainer. "Tate called me an old geezer. That's when I knew the possibility was there."

"Old geezer, huh?" Anna crossed one bare foot over the other. "What tipped you over?"

"Lots of little things." The way she'd bossed him around when they decorated his tree, insisting the star went on last. The way she'd pulled her dignity together in front of his parents while wearing a shirt that was a half-inch too short to completely cover her assets. The way she looked at him—as if she'd never seen anyone quite so fantastic.

And because she'd ruined him for anyone else. He'd never find another Tate in the world, no matter how hard he looked. She was one of a kind.

He'd talked to her about starting new Christmas traditions. He'd encouraged her to have fun. He'd led her to believe that it would be easy. Then, when the opportunity arose, he'd taken the easy way out, because letting go of happy memories to make way for new ones was hard.

She'd told him to go home for Christmas and enjoy it with family. He should have read between the lines. He should have known better. He should have stayed in Grand to be there for her, helping her start over, because for her, there was no easy way out.

He was having a great time with family. Meanwhile, she and Ford were doing their best to survive Christmas with only each other.

He'd let her down.

"The Christmas present she gave Iris," he said, in response to Anna's question. "It's a picture she took of Iris and me together. We're smiling at each other, and Iris has her hand on my cheek." He tapped the scar on his face. "It reminds me that the important people in my life can see past this and still find me pretty."

"I like her already." Anna's face—so much like his own, except for the scar—softened. He liked the way she looked at him, too. "When do I get to meet her?"

"I'm not sure," he said.

"Want to hear my suggestion?"

"Do I have a choice?"

Anna could be persistent when she made her mind up about something. She flapped her hand for him to be silent. "Don't let Mom dictate your life." Which was a little— scratch that, a lot—like the pot calling the kettle a spade. "Why not go get Tate the day after Christmas and bring her here for the rest of the week?"

Why not?

"That idea isn't half bad," he said.

But it wasn't quite right.

When they returned to the family room to join the others, it was the scene of either happy chaos or a crime, depending on the perspective. Dad and Neil sipped beer while shooting pool and dodging the building blocks littering the floor. His mom protected Iris while Pax entertained them with his new truck. The cornered tree cringed in terror. Sydney, with the exuberance of a five-year-old Mariah Carey super fan but none of the talent, danced around the room, mangling the lyrics to "All I want for Christmas is You." She had the sentiment down pat, if not the words.

Tate would love this. She thrived on chaos.

And suddenly, Miles knew what he wanted for Christmas. He wasn't waiting for the day after to get it, either.

He was going to go home and collect it right now.

"I have to make a phone call," he said.

HE CROSSED COUNTY lines and drove into Grand a few hours ahead of the storm. Snow had already begun falling as he'd left the airport in Billings, but so far, the ground in Grand remained bare. Weather reports stated that it would be a white Christmas after all.

Leaving Iris in Texas hadn't been easy, but his mom and his sister had kicked up such a fuss when he said he was taking her with him that he'd given in. Let them have her this once. Next year he'd be properly settled in Grand, and he wasn't budging.

He stopped at his house to drop off his suitcase and the fixings for tomorrow's Christmas dinner. While he was there, he wrapped Ford's gift and slid it under the tree, because both Shannahans were invited. Of course. He'd arranged for Tate's gift to be delivered to the ranch, which was where he was taking her as soon as he picked her up.

He changed his clothes and got in his truck. When he was a few minutes away, he called her number and drummed his thumb on the steering wheel while he waited for her to answer. Butterflies bucked in his chest.

This had better go over the way he hoped.

Tate

THE TREE LIGHTS were on and a few fat lazy snowflakes

fluttered past the living room window. The turkey thawed in the fridge. The trailer was as cozy as Tate could make it and Ford was in an unusually good mood. He'd been gone all morning. This afternoon he was holed up in his bedroom, claiming he had something to wrap, being all mysterious about it.

And yet something was missing.

Two somethings, in fact. A soon-to-be nine-month-old and her daddy.

Tate's ringtone pealed out "The Rodeo Song," and her funk disappeared. She answered, anxious to hear how Miles's trip to Texas was going and if Iris had settled in, determined she wouldn't ruin things for him by letting on how much she missed them.

"*You better watch out, you better not cry… Santa Claus is coming to town,*" Miles's voice boomed in her ear.

Tate collapsed on the sofa in giggles while he sang the whole song.

"You nut," she gasped out when he was finished.

"Would it be wrong of me to ask what you're wearing?"

She contemplated her sweatpants and fuzzy slippers. "It wouldn't be wrong, only disappointing for you." Someone knocked on the door. She waited to see if Ford would get it, but either he hadn't heard, or he was too busy. "Hang on a second. There's someone at the door."

She scrambled off the sofa and opened the door. She gaped.

It was Santa.

"Ho, ho, ho," Santa said. He tucked his cell phone in his pocket. "I'm here to find out who's naughty or nice."

Tate leaned on the doorframe. "The last Santa who tried that line with me got an answer he didn't expect."

Santa waggled his eyebrows in a jolly but un-Christmassy way. "I'm a hot Santa. I'm counting on getting a different reaction."

"You most definitely are. And you most definitely will." Tate threw her arms around his neck and kissed him, then scrubbed at her tingling lips with the back of her hand. "The beard tickles, though. You should shave." She peered past his shoulder and tried to see inside his truck, which already had a light dusting of snow on the hood. "Where's your elf?"

"I gave her this Christmas Eve off. She's at the North Pole with her grandma and auntie until the day after tomorrow when you and I go to collect her. I figured she wouldn't know the difference if Christmas in Grand came a day or two late."

"I'm not sure I know what's going on right now," Tate confessed.

"And I plan to keep it that way for a little while longer. Go get your coat and boots on." Santa looked at the sky. "We don't have long before this snow turns into a whiteout."

Tate called out to Ford to let him know she was leaving, then followed Miles to his truck.

He backed out of the yard and turned toward the Endeavour, not the town. The tires left white tracks in the road, but it wasn't snowing hard enough yet for the windshield wipers to stay on.

"Why are we going to the ranch?" Tate asked.

"You'll see."

Ford wasn't the only person being mysterious today. Tate was too happy to care. Being with Miles was all that mattered to her, and nothing could top that.

They turned into the Endeavour Ranch, but Miles didn't stop at the house, rather kept driving until they reached one of the barns. He unhooked his beard, tossing it and his Santa hat into the back seat.

The barn was dusty and warm inside, and filled with the smells of horse, oiled leather, and hay. Ryan O'Connell raised Tennessee Walkers and Tate had brought Iris in here a few times to admire them. Horses were the one thing about rodeos that she missed.

Miles didn't stop at the first stalls but headed straight down the barn's center aisle until he reached the far end. Tate blinked a few times, unsure of what she was seeing, then blinked a little more to clear the tears from her eyes.

"It's Davey," she said, reaching out to rub the mare's familiar soft, velvety nose. "Did you buy me my horse for Christmas?"

"Of course not," Miles said. "You can't afford to stable a horse on the little bit of money I pay you. That would be a terrible gift. I bought her for myself. Merry Christmas to me."

Tate would have laughed, but she was too busy getting a pat down from Davey that felt more like a mugging.

"Mind you," Miles continued, appearing to enjoy the crime currently in progress as much as Tate was, "I'll need someone to exercise her for me. Fortunately, you'll be working at the ranch every day. That's why I ordered you a new saddle for Christmas."

"Thank you," Tate said. Her eyes were still stinging. "How did you ever manage this? You couldn't possibly have known how to find her."

"Ford might have had a hand in it."

Which explained her brother's good mood. She was glad she'd bought him that new camera he'd been eyeing, even if it did cost more than her car.

She spent the next twenty minutes talking to Davey while brushing her coat. Miles leaned on the rail, seeming content to watch her hijack the gift he'd bought for himself.

"I hate to cut this reunion short," he finally said, "but you two can get reacquainted later. The snow's really coming down and we've got to get home."

"You Texas boys and your phobias about snow," Tate complained, but she put the brush down. She slid her hand into his as they retraced their steps through the barn.

Miles gave her fingers a squeeze, then bumped her shoulder with his. "Look at you, getting all friendly with Santa."

"Wait until you find out how friendly I'm willing to be. And how naughty I am."

"Well, Merry Christmas to me yet again. Ford, by the way, said he'd come by in the morning. He didn't appear interested in any Christmas Eve traditions we might want to start. His exact words were, 'If I don't know what you do to my sister, then I don't have to kill you.'"

"That's sweet," Tate said. "He gave you a present."

They cleared soft, thick snow off the truck, then Miles started the engine. The radio sprang to life and Rascal Flatts sang out, "I'll be home for Christmas."

Miles reached for the control. "Let's find something a touch more upbeat."

Tate stopped him. "No." She wanted to remember why she'd been so sad as the season approached. She wanted to believe that her twin was reaching out to remind her of how he'd always be with her. She wanted to trust that no matter how hard life got, there were always bends and twists in the road that led to better things. "It's a beautiful song." And a lovely version of it.

Miles waited until the song was over, then leaned over and kissed her. "I love you, Tate."

Tate put her whole heart into kissing him back. As much as she loved Davey, she loved Miles more. He'd returned for her, and that gift was priceless. She brought her fingers to the scar on his cheek, stroking the ridges and bumps, admiring the texture that represented all that he was—sensitive and tender and tough where he needed to be.

"I've had a crush on Miles Decker since I was fifteen years old. Then I met you, and saw you with Iris, and realized how much more amazing you are in real life. And I fell in love with you both."

That sounded so inadequate, given the depth of her feelings, but as usual, Miles understood. "I hope I don't disappoint you."

The concern in his eyes made her love him a hundred times more. "You haven't so far." Snow threatened to bury the windshield again. Miles's sunny Texas concerns over the turn in the weather weren't completely unfounded. Grand's Christmas was going to be white and likely several feet deep. Fortunately, it hadn't yet started to drift. "Possibly millions of kids around the world, but me? I'm about to be snowbound with Hot Santa. How lucky can a girl get?"

Miles shot her the smile that set her heart pounding—the one reserved for her, not his fans—and shifted the truck into gear.

"Let's go home and find out."

Epilogue

Miles

TATE STILL WASN'T a big fan of Christmas, despite Miles's best efforts, and he hated seeing the sadness creep into her eyes as the season approached. She'd been distracted.

That was why this year, their first as a cohabiting couple, he hoped to shake up the pattern, work on those new traditions, and put the joy back into her world, once and for all. He'd started with the neighborhood light competition. He'd lit up the house and yard to the point she'd informed him NASA had called to ask that he scale it back because it interfered with satellite imaging from space. The McIntyres hadn't stood a chance.

It was also why he'd indulged her and was out in a snow-storm, participating in the scavenger hunt she'd set up for him and Ford. Ford, the cagey bastard, had insisted on traveling solo. Miles wouldn't put it past him to head for home, where it was comfy and warm and a whole lot more fun than this, instead.

The first stop on Tate's itinerary was the hospital. He found the note she'd wrapped in plastic and taped to the underside of a trash bin lid, instructing him to head for the church next. Thank Saint Nick for four-wheel drive transmissions and snow tires because the roads were drifting in fast.

The instructions at the church were taped to the door, under the wreath.

Muttering curses at Christmas spirits, his third stop was the daycare in the center of Grand. After that was the elementary school, then the high school. The final stop was the nursing home, where the note at the nursing station inside sent him back to the house.

Okay…

He'd figured it out. Tate had wanted to get him out from under her feet for a few hours. Now he was intrigued. And cold. And not quite as obliging as he'd been when he started.

"Your brother had better be here," he called out to her, stomping the snow off his boots at the door. "Because I'm not going out looking for him."

"He called to say the storm was getting worse and he was spending the night at the taproom," Tate replied from the kitchen. "Come have some mulled cider."

Miles squeezed past the tree. He'd refused to downsize but was willing to negotiate a larger house in the future. He entered the kitchen, still his favorite room, and found his

213

two favorite ladies. Tate, looking festive in a red T-shirt, green leggings, and a pair of his thick gray wool socks, stood at the stove and ladled hot spiced cider into a mug. The spicy scents of ginger and cloves hung in the air. Iris played on the floor with pots and pans and the remote for the stereo system. Her T-shirt and leggings matched Tate's.

He forgot all about being annoyed by the wild-goose scavenger chase, because this was why he'd been so eager to start new traditions in his own home. Coming home to his family—to the two people he loved most in the world—was better than any rush that bull riding could give him.

"What was that little expedition all about?" he asked as he accepted the steaming mug of cider from her and dropped a kiss on her mouth. She tasted of sugar and spice and everything nice.

"You'll figure it out soon enough."

Her mysterious tone sparked his interest. Something was up.

"Should I check the bedroom?" Because good things happened there.

"Not until after Iris goes to bed," she said, dashing his hopes.

The storm rattled the windows as snow piled up against the glass garden door overlooking the winter wonderland of the back yard. "Where should I look?"

"Right here in the kitchen. My God, Miles. You are such a man." Tate was laughing. Even Iris was grinning at him, showing off pearly baby teeth, obviously in on whatever the joke was.

He checked the cupboards. Nothing new there. Then the fridge and inside the oven. Every corner. Meanwhile, Tate was in tears from laughing so hard.

"I give up," he said. "Maybe you could give me a hint."

"Think about all the places I sent you. You started at the hospital. Then the daycare…" She trailed off as if expecting him to piece it together from that tiny scrap of information.

He looked at her. He looked again. And he stared at the front of her T-shirt, which read, BABY ON BOARD. His heart began pounding. He spun around to check out Iris's T-shirt. It said, I'LL BE A BIG SISTER IN JULY.

He grew light-headed and had to grab hold of the island to steady himself. They'd never really discussed giving Iris a little brother or sister, but they'd gotten lax about birth control. He couldn't recall when the box of condoms next to the bed had last been replaced.

And until this very second, he hadn't realized how much he regretted not being a part of Iris's birth. He'd missed out on the months of anticipation, and the labor and delivery. He hadn't gotten to bring her home from the hospital or experience the terror-filled days of learning what it meant to have complete responsibility for a fragile human life. He hadn't gotten to see a lot of her firsts, either—the first time she smiled, the first time she rolled over, the first time she sat up on her own. If he had one regret where she was concerned, it was that she wasn't the result of two people loving each other.

Not the way this new baby would be.

"Are you okay with this?" Tate asked, sounding anxious, no longer laughing, and he realized he was ruining her big Christmas Moment.

His head cleared. "Am I *okay* with this this?" He lifted her off her feet and spun her around. "Sweetheart, *okay* doesn't begin to scratch the surface as to how I feel about this." He kissed her until they were both short of breath. "What was the nursing home all about, though?" he asked once he was sure he could speak without his voice cracking. "I hope there'll be a few more stages between high school and that."

Tate placed her hands on his face and rubbed her thumb against his scarred cheek, something he noticed she did whenever she was pulling her feelings together in an attempt to explain them.

"The stages in between won't be ours. Those belong to Iris and whoever this is," she said, dropping one hand to her stomach. "They'll have to go out on their own at some point and we'll have to accept it. It's where we are with our families, right now."

Where they were with his family was good, but with her parents wasn't great. Miles found it hard to get past the way they'd checked out on Tate and Ford, as if they'd only had one child who mattered—but that relationship was between the Shannahans, and he'd mind his own business.

"You have no idea how much I love you right now," he said, turning back to the moment. "But did you really need to send me out in a snowstorm for three hours just to put on a T-shirt?"

"I trusted you to have enough sense to get off the roads if you didn't think it was safe." Tate hugged him around the waist and kissed him. "There might be something special in the bedroom for you this evening to make up for it," she added. She looked at him in that way that made him feel 100 percent pretty and like the luckiest man in the world. She didn't need to say it to let him know he how much he was loved.

Three Dog Night launched into "Joy to the World" at the tops of their lungs. Iris dropped the stereo remote. Her startled expression had them both laughing.

"Merry Christmas," Tate said.

Best Christmas ever.

The End

Want more? Check out Dan and Jasmine's story in
The Montana Sheriff!

Join Tule Publishing's newsletter for more great reads and weekly deals!

If you enjoyed *The Cowboy's Christmas Baby*, you'll love the other books in…

The Endeavour Ranch of Grand, Montana series

Book 1: *The Montana Sheriff*

Book 2: *The Montana Doctor*

Book 3: *The Montana Rancher*

Book 4: *The Cowboy's Christmas Baby*

Available now at your favorite online retailer!

More Books by Paula Altenburg

The Montana McGregor Brothers series

Book 1: *The Rancher Takes a Family*

Book 2: *The Rancher's Secret Love*

Book 3: *The Rancher's Proposal*

A Sweetheart Brand series

Book 1: *Her Montana Brand*

Book 2: *The Cowboy's Brand*

Book 3: *Branded by the Cowboy*

Available now at your favorite online retailer!

About the Author

USA Today Bestselling Author Paula Altenburg lives in rural Nova Scotia, Canada with her husband and two sons. A former aviation and aerospace professional, Paula now writes contemporary romance and fantasy with romantic elements.

Thank you for reading

The Cowboy's Christmas Baby

If you enjoyed this book, you can find more from all our
great authors at TulePublishing.com, or from your favorite
online retailer.

TULE
PUBLISHING

Made in the USA
Las Vegas, NV
12 November 2023

80721715R00135